'You come **before dawn o** **and ask a wo** **your child.**

'How did you expect her to take it?'

He shifted as if the chair had suddenly become too small for him. 'As a bit of a joke?' he hazarded.

'Only it wasn't,' Daisy reminded him, provoking a long drawn-out sigh and more running of fingers through the dark hair. 'Was it?'

He shook his head.

'It seemed so simple when I started to think about it. All I had to do was find a woman who wanted children and didn't find me totally repulsive, and in return I'd offer her a home, whatever help she wanted or needed, financial security, companionship—'

'Regular sex?'

He looked so startled she laughed. 'Well, you need to go a bit further than companionship to have a child.'

Was he blushing? Surely not!

Dear Reader

Over the last few years I've really enjoyed reading 'relationship' books involving the lives of young, single career women juggling priorities to find enough time for love, friendship, shopping and even basic personal maintenance. Generally, the support network of other single friends keeps them sane, so the idea of helping four friends find love really appealed to me.

Gabi, Kirsten, Alana and Daisy all live in the Near West apartment building, and work or have worked at the Royal Westside Hospital. Gabi, a doctor, has loved and lost. Kirsten, an occupational therapist, has been held in the grip of unrequited love. Nurse Alana's previous venture into romance has left her preferring the company of her pets; though she strongly believes in love, she theorises that it grows from friendship, not attraction. Daisy is a psychologist, who can tell them why things happen as they do, but can't quite sort out her own problems.

The four friends share each other's tears and laughter, and, often with unexpected consequences, try to help each other along the rocky road to love.

I have had such fun getting to know these women as I wrote these four books, and I hope you enjoy their company as much as I have.

Meredith Webber

Recent titles by the same author:

THE DOCTOR'S DESTINY (Alana's story)
DEAR DOCTOR (Kirsten's story)
DR GRAHAM'S MARRIAGE (Gabi's story)

DAISY AND THE DOCTOR

BY
MEREDITH WEBBER

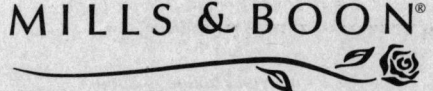

DID YOU PURCHASE THIS BOOK WITHOUT A COVER?

If you did, you should be aware it is **stolen property** as it was reported *unsold and destroyed* by a retailer. Neither the author nor the publisher has received any payment for this book.

All the characters in this book have no existence outside the imagination of the author, and have no relation whatsoever to anyone bearing the same name or names. They are not even distantly inspired by any individual known or unknown to the author, and all the incidents are pure invention.

All Rights Reserved including the right of reproduction in whole or in part in any form. This edition is published by arrangement with Harlequin Enterprises II B.V. The text of this publication or any part thereof may not be reproduced or transmitted in any form or by any means, electronic or mechanical, including photocopying, recording, storage in an information retrieval system, or otherwise, without the written permission of the publisher.

This book is sold subject to the condition that it shall not, by way of trade or otherwise, be lent, resold, hired out or otherwise circulated without the prior consent of the publisher in any form of binding or cover other than that in which it is published and without a similar condition including this condition being imposed on the subsequent purchaser.

MILLS & BOON and MILLS & BOON with the Rose Device are registered trademarks of the publisher.

*First published in Great Britain 2003
Harlequin Mills & Boon Limited,
Eton House, 18-24 Paradise Road, Richmond, Surrey TW9 1SR*

© Meredith Webber 2003

ISBN 0 263 83436 0

*Set in Times Roman 10½ on 12 pt.
03-0403-50808*

*Printed and bound in Spain
by Litografia Rosés, S.A., Barcelona*

CHAPTER ONE

THE phone call came as Daisy was lying on her bed, staring at the ceiling and wondering if she'd made the worst mistake of her life when she'd told the radio station that ran her talk-back psychology show she was quitting.

True, she had a part-time temporary job starting Monday, and still had her interactive web-site, but the radio show that had been her life for so long was now someone else's baby.

Baby!

Oh, dear! Was she game? Would she go through with this mad idea? *Could* she do it?

The idea of a baby snuggled warmly beneath her breast. *Her* baby! A child to whom she could give all the love she'd been denied—all the love that filled her heart to overflowing but presently had no outlet, other than her cyber-patients.

But was single parenthood fair on the baby?

Better than some alternatives, surely...

Awash in a sea of confusion, she reached for the receiver with all the relief of a shipwrecked sailor reaching for a lifebelt. Anything to stop thinking.

'Hello!'

'Daisy, it's Gabi. I'm sorry to phone you so early but I'm up in the penthouse. You know Madeleine and Graham Frost are away?'

Without waiting for a response, Gabi Graham, a neighbour from the fourth floor of the Near West building where Daisy lived, rushed on. 'And Ingrid's throwing a fit, says she's leaving, and as she packs she's alternately cursing both Madeleine and Madeleine's brother Julian, who's here while the Frosts are away. Well, I think that's what she's doing, it's mostly in Swedish—and she's talking about cows. She said "cows" in English, but maybe it's a Swedish word as well and she's not talking about real cows.'

Daisy stifled a giggle as she pictured the scene, which must be hilarious, given the usually calm Gabi's flustered reaction to the beautiful Swedish nanny's volatility.

'I have to go to work,' Gabi said, more hesitant now.

There was a moment's pause before she added, 'And you do know Ingrid better than the rest of us, so I wondered...'

'I'll have a quick shower then come right up,' Daisy promised. 'You get off to work.'

At least it would stop her thinking about the job she'd so recently left.

And about the other life-altering decision she'd made. The one which had prompted the resignation.

But as she showered, her mind wasn't on either her job or the hysterical nanny but on Ingrid's charges, the twin boys, Shaun and Ewan.

She blotted water from her body with a towel, hoping someone had had the forethought to move them away from the scene of the drama, while her heart ached as she considered the upheaval Ingrid's departure would mean in their young lives.

The only reason she knew Ingrid—and the twins—reasonably well was because she'd often accompanied the threesome to a nearby park for the sheer joy of seeing the two children running, laughing, fighting and playing.

Surrogate children, she knew, but all she'd thought to have in her life until recently—when she'd made the momentous but still rational decision to stop working nights, stabilise her life and have a child of her own.

The thought, though she'd now had many weeks while she'd finished up at the radio station, to get used to it, still caused her stomach to cramp with a swirly cocktail of anxiety and excitement, so she had to blank it out—deliberately forcing her attention onto the plight of the twins. How would they react to the departure of their nanny at a time when both their parents were away?

Pulling on the first clothes that came to hand, a pair of calf-length white denim pants and an over-large, vivid pink lightweight Indian cotton shirt, she paused only long enough to drag a brush through her mass of unruly black hair—not that it made much difference what she did to it, it always sprang back to its wild and untamed ways within minutes.

She had to stop Ingrid leaving—it was the only answer.

As if it had known she'd need it, the lift was on her floor—the second—and she stepped in and pressed the button for the fifth floor. The doors opened into a foyer that only served the penthouse and Gabi, perhaps hearing the ping of the lift's arrival, was at the door to greet her.

The background noise was such that speech was impossible, so Gabi made do with grabbing Daisy's hand and dragging her into the big apartment.

'I've got to go,' she said, above the din. 'Good luck.'

Daisy watched her dash away, then shut her eyes for a moment, gathering strength to wade into the fray.

'Hello!' she called, because it seemed slightly rude to walk in totally unannounced.

No one answered, so she followed the noise, bypassing a room where Ingrid was flinging clothes into a suitcase and muttering Swedish imprecations and on to the next room, the twins' domain.

It had been set up for two separate functions, the first part being an open playroom, then, through an arch hung with colourful mobiles and small soft toys on bright ribbons, a smaller sleeping area.

In the middle of the first area, sitting on a very small chair at a very small table, was a very large man.

Daisy took in a shock of dark hair, straighter but almost as unruly as her own mop, with a few random streaks of grey already running through it. But apart from that, and his size, she didn't notice much, her attention diverted by the sight of the twins, both of whom, though now close to three years old, were throwing textbook two-year-old tantrums. The small bodies were face down on the floor, legs and arms flailing, red faces awash with tears while roars of disapproval erupted from their tiny throats.

The big man turned towards her.

'I tried placating them and when that didn't work I decided to ignore them,' he said, turning towards Daisy so she saw his face properly for the first time. It was an amiable face, though presently marred by a concerned frown, but she couldn't see any anger in the hazel eyes which, even in these circumstances, appeared to hold the hint of a smile. 'I presume you're Daisy.'

'Ignoring them doesn't seem to be working either,' Daisy pointed out, but he didn't seem perturbed by her criticism.

She sat down on the floor and lifted the closest of the screaming children on to her lap. It was Shaun, though if anyone had asked her how she knew she couldn't have explained.

'Hush, little one,' she murmured, rocking him in her arms and edging closer so she could touch Ewan at the same time. 'You're upsetting Ewan with your crying. Look at him! See how unhappy he is. And look at Uncle Julian, sitting on your chair. Doesn't he look silly? Would you like to sit with him while I give Ewan a cuddle?'

She was talking to calm and soothe him, nothing more, her voice low and soft so he had to quieten to hear it. The suggestion that he sit with Uncle Julian didn't go down well, causing two small but chubby arms to tighten around her neck.

'OK, so you stay on my knee but make room for Ewan,' she suggested, settling Shaun on one knee and lifting the other little boy off the floor.

His tantrum had subsided into a series of sobs and hiccups, and within seconds the pair were kicking each other and getting bits of Daisy as they did so.

'That's enough now,' Daisy said firmly, then still holding them against her body, she said, 'Stop crying and tell me what's the matter.'

'Wrong question,' the big man murmured.

As if she needed telling when both children were wailing again, though this time there were stifled attempts to explain.

'Hush up, I can't think while you're being so noisy.'

She jiggled them up and down as best she could, glad they weren't triplets, then as the wails weakened to sniffles and heart-wrenching sobs she said, 'What if you two play quietly in here and I'll go and have a talk to Ingrid?'

'Good luck!' The dryly uttered words whispered through the air, while the twins snuggled closer to Daisy as if their places in her lap were the only safe haven in an increasingly disturbing world.

'I can't talk to her while I'm sitting here,' she said, easing first Shaun, and then Ewan, onto the carpet before crawling over to pull a big plastic garage towards them. 'Here, we can play with this. Uncle Julian can get some more cars off the shelves.'

She directed the words towards the man, hoping he'd hear the command in her voice and do something more than provide a running commentary on the situation.

He rose to his feet with surprising grace, given his size and his starting point on the miniature chair, and crossed to the open shelves that lined the wall, selecting small cars and trucks with deliberate concentration.

Uncle Julian! The twins had talked of no one else when they and Madeleine had returned from a holiday with their uncle. He'd been living and working in London, and some time ago, when Ingrid had suffered a severe injury to her leg, Madeleine had insisted on flying the young woman home to Stockholm to convalesce while she and the twins had stayed with Julian in London.

Now Uncle Julian was here.

Right here, in fact, kneeling beside her and placing cars on various levels of the garage, making zooming noises as he spun them down ramps and enticing the twins into joining the game.

This close he was even larger than he'd seemed on the chair—not an overweight kind of large, just *there* somehow. Taking up more room than normal human beings, and in some strange manner consuming more than his share of available air, so she felt slightly breathless.

'Julian Austin,' he said, formally introducing himself while still zooming cars around the garage.

'Daisy Rutherford,' Daisy responded, studying the man's face—dark eyebrows dominating a wide brow, a strong nose, just sufficiently out of kilter to be interesting and lips neither thick nor thin but wide enough to give the impression he was always on the verge of smiling.

'Do you know what's upset Ingrid?'

The smile thing happened again, lips twisting so it was rueful rather than amused, and he looked directly at her, revealing eyes the colour of the deep water at the end of the pier at the beach where she'd holidayed as a child. A mix of blue and green with glints of the gold where sunlight sparkled—not that eyes could look like the ocean.

'I think it was me asking her if she'd like to have my baby,' he said, little lines fanning out around the mesmerising eyes as the rueful smile widened and actually lit what looked suspiciously like a twinkle in the colour-changing depths.

'Oh, really?' Daisy scoffed, certain he was joking. 'Silly girl! You'd have thought she'd have jumped at the chance.'

Julian Austin nodded solemnly and, with the smile and twinkle gone, Daisy realised the man was serious.

'You *are* joking?' she demanded, unable to believe her instinct.

He looked surprised and shrugged as if he didn't understand her question.

'Why would I be?'

He *wasn't* joking.

'Because you don't just walk into someone's house and ask the nanny to have your baby? It's—it's…'

She couldn't think of the word but his response certainly wasn't the expression she was looking for.

'Not done?' her companion queried quietly. 'But it's a sensible arrangement and I thought she knew.'

Daisy closed her eyes and took a deep breath, then

cautiously opened them again to check she hadn't slid into a parallel universe.

She hadn't, but breathing deeply had obviously got her brain working again.

'You've known her a while? You've been courting her long-distance?' She put her assumptions into words. 'Perhaps you should have proposed more romantically. You know, the "I love you and want to marry you" approach. It's less abrupt and just a tad more romantic than "I want you to have my baby".'

The big man shifted, no doubt because kneeling had become uncomfortable. He shuffled until he was sitting, legs stretched away from Daisy although the rest of him was still close.

'But I don't. Love her, that is. I mean, we barely know each other. I've only been here two days, so how could I possibly love her? And that's granting such a concept as romantic love exists outside commercial advertising, which I doubt. Not once a person is over the hormonal upheaval of adolescence anyway. But Madeleine had told me Ingrid wanted to marry a doctor, and I'm a doctor, so it seemed about right. And from the way Madeleine spoke, I thought she'd already suggested it to Ingrid and had sorted out the finer details so, of course, when I saw how good she was with the twins the words just popped out.'

'Of course,' Daisy echoed weakly. 'You say Madeleine had sorted it out?' This was even more unbelievable, as Madeleine usually flitted through life from one terribly important social engagement to the next, upkeep visits to the beauty parlour and her favourite hairdresser squeezed in between.

Daisy wouldn't have put her top of a list of people to arrange someone else's marriage.

Not even halfway down!

However, now wasn't the time to be criticising Madeleine's lifestyle or her ability as a marriage broker. Neither was there time to point out to Julian his gross insensitivity—not if she wanted to stop Ingrid's departure. Shaking her head in disbelief, Daisy stood up, and headed for Ingrid's bedroom.

'Ingrid!' She tapped on the door although it was open, and watched the lovely blonde ignore the intrusion as she snapped shut the last clasp on her suitcase. 'May I come in?'

Ingrid shrugged as if the matter was sublimely immaterial to her.

'Ingrid, talk to me. Tell me what's wrong. We'll sort it out. You can't go off and leave the twins like this.'

'I'm going,' Ingrid announced, shifting one case to the floor then proceeding to hurl small personal items into the one still on the bed. 'Madeleine has betrayed me.'

'Madeleine? I thought it was Julian who upset you.'

Ingrid spun towards Daisy, her eyes flaring with anger.

'He, too!' she growled. 'But it is Madeleine who betrayed me, who thought to make me breeding cow. I will *not* mind her children.'

Breeding cow? Gabi had been right about the animal references.

'We say brood mare—horses, not cows.' Daisy made the correction automatically, as part of their time together in the park had always included an incidental English lesson. 'What did Madeleine do?'

'Told her brother I have his baby—breeding mare, see?'

Daisy was sorry she'd asked. Far from providing any

rational explanation, Ingrid's replies were confusing the issue.

'You must have got it wrong,' Daisy said firmly, although Julian had said much the same thing—or had implied it when he'd said he'd asked Ingrid to have his baby.

But surely—

'Anyway, I want to go. I told Madeleine I wanted to go. I can earn good money in Japan, being a model hostess in fancy restaurant. My friends already do this.'

Daisy remembered hearing something about this idea—remembered Madeleine being horrified after Ingrid had been approached in a shopping centre by someone who, in Madeleine's eyes, was little more than a white-slave trader. Gabi and Alana had tried to reassure Madeleine but apparently she'd not believed them and had dreamed up this idea of marrying Ingrid off to her brother. No doubt so she wouldn't have to train another nanny!

'But it's a strange country, with another language to learn, and it's very expensive to live there.'

Daisy almost smiled as she added this last bit of information, certain it would sway the other woman. Ingrid was very careful about money.

'The owners of restaurant have flat and I can give English lessons as well to make more money.'

This time Daisy did smile, but swallowed it quickly in case Ingrid saw and was offended. *More* offended.

'But what about the twins? They'll be devastated if you leave, especially now with Madeleine away. Couldn't you stay until she and Graham come back? It's only four weeks.'

Ingrid shook her head, but at least had the grace to

look embarrassed about letting down the couple who had been very good to her.

'The job is for now, not in four weeks,' she muttered, and Daisy's sympathy turned to anger.

'You did this deliberately. You waited until Madeleine was gone so she wouldn't try to talk you out of it. It had nothing to do with Julian.'

Ingrid turned fierce blue eyes on her.

'It did. I would have stayed—got another job in Japan later.'

But the eyes wavered, not quite meeting Daisy's, leaving Daisy to suspect her assumptions were correct. Not that she'd tell Julian Austin. As long as he believed he was guilty of chasing Ingrid away, he'd be more diligent in the care of his nephews.

'This is my address for Madeleine to send the money she will owe me.'

Ingrid shoved a piece of paper into Daisy's hand, then gathered up some documents, including what looked suspiciously like an airline ticket, from the bed. She tucked these into her handbag and slung its strap over her shoulder, then lifted both her cases and walked out of the bedroom.

'Great!' Daisy muttered to herself, but she followed Ingrid out, then hurried ahead of her to open the front door.

'Shouldn't you at least say goodbye to the twins?' she said, as Ingrid dropped her cases in the foyer and summoned the lift.

For the first time Ingrid's composure cracked, and tears pooled in her eyes.

'It would make me too sad,' she said. 'They were like my children, but they were not my children. It is not good, being nanny.'

Daisy understood. She hugged the now quietly weeping young woman and wished her luck, helped her carry her cases into the lift, then watched the doors close.

'Well, that was helpful!'

She turned to see Julian watching from the door of the apartment.

'She had her plane ticket—nothing was going to stop her going,' Daisy told him.

'And a cab waiting downstairs. The cabbie just phoned up from the lobby.' He ran his fingers through his hair, making it even more untidy than it had been. 'She was going anyway?'

So much for using guilt to ensure he took good care of the twins!

'Apparently,' Daisy agreed, but she had no intention of letting him off the hook too easily. 'Though you definitely precipitated the crisis. Why on earth would you ask a woman you barely know to have your baby?'

Shaun's arrival with a demand that Uncle Julian return to the playroom diverted the man's attention, but as he walked away, slightly bent so he could hold his small nephew's hand, he glanced back and said, 'Because I really need at least one child.' He lifted Shaun into his arms and settled him on his hip then turned to add, 'Two or three would probably be better but as it's hard to produce twins or triplets on demand, I'd be happy to start with one.'

He continued towards the playroom so Daisy was forced to follow if she wanted to sort out this bizarre situation.

'It's easier for women who decide they want a family,' he continued, as if they were discussing the weather, or politics, or religion—a normal conversation! 'Because they actually carry the child, so all they have to do, should they decide they want a baby, is either find a man to impregnate them or find a sperm donor and do the deed in a less physical fashion.'

Definitely a parallel universe, Daisy decided. And to think she'd always thought science fiction shows totally unbelievable. They were back in the playroom now, Julian squatting on the floor with the two boys, playing cars, but continuing what must, to him, seem a perfectly logical discussion.

Why else would he be continuing?

'But a man needs a woman willing to do the actual carrying of the child, and if possible the early nurturing. I also believe a child is better off with two parents, so I thought marriage...' He turned his head towards Daisy, perhaps to make sure she was listening, then added, 'To make things legal and comfortable for the children, but marriage as a partnership of mutual convenience for the parents. I'm not too repulsive, I'm clean living, a non-smoker, I enjoy an occasional beer or glass of wine but I'm not so desperate I couldn't give that up if my partner objected, and I make a good living, or I should do once I'm established in the practice I'm buying. In some circles I'm what might be considered a good catch.'

He removed a car Ewan was trying to wedge into his mouth and kept talking, as if anxious to convince Daisy he wasn't mad.

So far he wasn't doing too well!

'It's the practice, you see. Male obstetricians have never had a baby, most orthopods have never had a knee replacement, neurosurgeons don't have to have had a brain tumour—'

'OK, I get the picture—you don't have to have experienced the problem to be able to treat it. But where are you going with this?'

'Just that it's different for paediatricians, and—'

'You're a paediatrician?'

This time he ignored Daisy's interruption.

'It's all very well telling people how they should bring up their children, and what they should and shouldn't do, but at some stage they invariably ask if I have any. And when I say no, their eyes take on a look of something very like contempt and I can see they immediately discount everything I've said to them. It's such a waste because I know I'm right about a lot of the things I tell them but, more often than not, they won't even give it a try because what would I know?'

Small glimmers of light began to flicker in the morass of confusion in Daisy's mind.

'What *do* you know?' she asked.

'Quite a lot,' he replied firmly, still with ninety per cent of his concentration on the car game and the twins. 'I've worked at some of the top children's hospitals all around the world, but have also done a lot of work with children with disabilities and with children who have behavioural problems—do you know anything about behaviour modification?'

'Just a smidgen,' Daisy said, and actually saw him start. His head swivelled towards her, the green-blue eyes revealing surprise and something else—embarrassment?

'Daisy Rutherford! I heard you say your name and it just didn't register.' He stood up and held out his hand and she took it automatically. 'I do apologise,' he added humbly. 'I had no idea. Typical of Madeleine not to tell me you lived in the building. I thought your paper on rewards and punishment was excellent. We've been going down the rewards and anti-negativity path for too long. There is a place for punishment but, as you pointed out, it has to be appropriate, non-abusive and tailored to fit the crime.'

'I'm sure I didn't use the word "crime",' Daisy protested, wondering why her hand was still resting in his grasp—and why she wasn't removing it.

Because it felt warm there—and safe somehow, though that was a ridiculous concept. She slid it away from his and tucked it firmly into one pocket so it wouldn't stray.

Pockets were safe!

'I'm sure you didn't. You're far too professional.' Julian beamed down at her. 'I always look out for your papers. I don't suppose *you'd* like to have my baby?'

It was a joke and Daisy knew it, but she *did* want a baby—she *had* already made that decision—and this man was obviously intelligent, he looked healthy, the twins were examples of good family genes...

'Actually, I might,' she said, and saw the shock of his reaction register on his face. Eager to explain, she rushed on. 'Well, I've just left work so I could have a child, but apart from making myself physically available—'

It wasn't until the words were out that she realised how they'd sounded. She clapped her hands to her cheeks to cool the rush of heat.

'I didn't mean it that way,' she gabbled. 'I mean I stopped working nights so—this is getting worse, isn't it?'

She looked desperately up at Julian, who, while undoubtedly bemused, was smiling kindly at her. Rather in the way he must smile at small but muddled patients.

'Take a deep breath and try again,' he suggested.

Daisy shook her head.

'No, thanks. I've made a big enough fool of myself

already. I'll just head back down to my flat and die of mortification.'

'Don't you dare!'

From kindly to authoritative in one breath!

'Die of mortification?' she teased, smiling to ease her own tension. 'I probably won't. I've been mortified by experts and survived.'

'I don't mean that!' Julian dismissed her chatter with a wave of his large hand. 'Don't you dare leave me is what I meant. With the twins. How can I cope? What am I supposed to do?'

'Look after them? Put some of your theories into practice?' She grinned at him. 'Think of the kudos it will give you with the parents of your patients.'

Thank heavens they were off the 'having a baby' subject. Hopefully, he'd be so occupied finding a new nanny, he'd forget it completely. Well, her part in it at least.

'I might manage over the weekend...' He paused, offering her a smile as he added, 'With your help. But I start work Monday. What do I do then?'

'You'll have to contact Madeleine. She might have used an emergency nanny service before. She'll tell you what to do.'

Julian shook his head, and for once the smile was missing, his face grave with concern.

'I don't want to tell her anything about it, if I can avoid it,' he said. 'Graham hasn't been well—he was sick for too long with a gastric bug he picked up when he was doing a month's voluntary surgery in the Pacific and now, though he won't admit it, he seems to have something very like chronic fatigue. Madeleine was hoping a long break away might be the answer.'

'Oh!' Daisy said, immediately feeling as concerned as

Julian looked. 'And if you phoned her, she'd come back—they both would.'

Julian nodded gloomily.

'What I need is some strategy so the twins are cared for, then Madeleine needn't know Ingrid's gone.'

'What about grandparents? Do you have an available mother—or does Graham's mother live nearby?'

'Grandparents. Now, why didn't I think of that? Will you watch them while I phone home?'

Daisy nodded, confident that once Julian was out of the room she'd be able to think straight. She sat down on the floor near the two boys and waited for the mental haze to clear, but instead of considering why she'd blurted out her 'Actually, I might' reply to Julian's ridiculous question, she found herself studying the boys...thinking about babies.

CHAPTER TWO

'MY MOTHER will be here early Monday morning. My father, too. They'll both come, as Dad has some business to attend to in Westside. Unfortunately, there's a bridge tournament Saturday and Sunday and as Mother's convinced everything will fall apart without her, they can't just walk away from it. But they'll drive down from the coast early Monday morning and should be here in time for me to leave for work.'

Julian's smile indicated how pleased he was with this news. But it was also cajoling, so Daisy wasn't surprised when he added, 'Do you think we can manage until then?'

'We?'

'You *will* help?' he said anxiously. 'When you can, of course. I realise you've got your own life to lead, and probably have all kinds of things to do over the weekend, but you said you're not working so if you have spare time…'

Daisy considered the plans she'd made for the weekend, but apart from a shopping trip to buy some suitable work clothes—she could hardly go back to work in a clinic in the comfortable but very casual clothes she wore around the house and to the radio station in the evenings—there wasn't a list of other exciting arrangements.

'I guess I can help you,' she said, and the smile Julian flashed her way made her regret her reluctant agreement.

'Great!' he said, with far too much enthusiasm, the

reason for which became apparent when he added, 'It means we can talk about the other business. The baby business.'

'There *is* no baby business,' Daisy said firmly, turning to play with the twins so the combination of shock and hurt he managed to portray on his expressive features couldn't influence her in any way.

'But you said, ''Actually, I might'',' he reminded her.

'That just slipped out,' Daisy said firmly. 'Because I *do* want to have a baby but, apart from us not knowing the slightest thing about each other, my baby wouldn't be any good to you as far as your work was concerned.'

He was frowning at her now.

'And why not?' he asked, moving to separate the twins to head off a fight over a small red fire truck. 'A baby's a baby after all.'

Daisy threw him an exasperated look.

'Because the whole point of you having a child is so you can be a hands-on father—have day-to-day experience of raising a child or children. But all I'm looking for is a sperm donor, and though I'd work out some kind of arrangement if the biological father wanted regular contact with the child, I'd be doing most of the parenting myself.'

Even as she spoke, Daisy found a small part of herself blinking in wonderment that she was having such an intimate conversation with a virtual stranger.

'You *want* to be a single parent?' Julian managed to convey such disbelief that Daisy felt a slow burn of anger flare to life in her chest.

'Why not?' she snapped at him. 'Are you going to tell me that children need two parents? We all know that's the ideal, but how often does it prove the best environment for the child? When the two parents fight all the time? When one or other changes partners at regular intervals, so instead of one father figure the child has six or seven? I don't intend getting pregnant accidentally then having to make the best of things later. I've planned this pregnancy, I've saved for it so I can spend those first formative years of my child's life with him or her. Look at all the children born to your ideal couples who are thrust into child-care when they're three months old because both parents work. Look at—'

'Hey!'

Julian touched her gently on the arm and, though it was no more than a brush of his fingers on her skin, she felt a tingle of awareness—or warning—flash along her nerves.

'I didn't mean you couldn't cope, or that most single parents don't handle their children beautifully, but I was thinking of the hassles and problems single parents encounter. You've probably got good family back-up, a mother who can step in if you're ill, and friends to support you at all times, but it's still a huge job.'

She could hear the concern in his voice and see it in his eyes, but mention of her mother had tightened the anxiety that had lurked beneath her bravado ever since she'd made her decision, and she dipped her head so he couldn't see her face—or guess at her wavering courage.

'The thing is,' he continued, after seating both boys at their small play table and providing them with wooden animal puzzles, 'you've probably never seriously considered an alternative to single parenthood. I mean, if there's no man in your life at present then you wouldn't have, would you?'

'Great! Now you're making me sound like a total loser,' Daisy said, straightening her spine and glaring at this aggravating man. 'I'll have you know there's no man in my life by choice.'

'I'm sure of that,' he agreed, helping Ewan turn a kangaroo so it would fit into the puzzle. 'You're a very attractive woman. But *have* you considered the alternative? An arrangement like the one I was going to offer Ingrid? A marriage of mutual convenience—like a business partnership?'

'No, and I don't intend to now,' Daisy snapped.

'But you must see how much easier it would be.' He turned another piece of puzzle. 'For a start, it would save you having to find your sperm donor. That can't be easy. How did you intend to go about it? Advertise?'

She peered suspiciously at him, sure he must be mocking her, but the smile wasn't in evidence and his eyes looked serious—interested, in fact. But his words still niggled, mainly because it was something she hadn't considered in depth though vague ideas had floated through her head from time to time.

'Something along the lines of, "Single loser needs sperm"?' she queried coldly. 'I'm not that desperate.'

She stood up. 'I'll go and get the boys some morning tea.'

And on that note she strode from the room, hoping Julian Austin would get the message that the subject was closed.

For ever.

'They're a pair of monsters,' Julian said, collapsing into a lounge chair and mopping his brow with a large white handkerchief.

It was one-thirty in the afternoon and the little boys had finally fallen asleep, but only after insisting that both Julian and Daisy read to them—in unison!

'They're taking advantage of us,' Daisy told him.

She was collapsed on the lounge opposite him, and had her feet propped on a coffee-table. If Madeleine didn't like her using it as a footstool, too bad!

'So, what do we do?'

Lazy eyelids rose, revealing the bright hazel eyes.

Daisy shrugged, then teased him with a smile.

'You're the expert.'

'But what I know is all theory—and I'm starting to feel as contemptuous of those theories as some parents do. That's why I need a family—kids of my own—so I can see what works and what doesn't.'

Oh, dear, back to that again. But in spite of herself, Daisy was intrigued.

'Have you something against the usual way of achieving this? You know, going out, meeting women, finding a particular woman to whom you're attracted, falling in love, marrying her and then having the children? I realise you're pushed for time, and think you need the children now, but what happens if the "falling in love with" woman comes along after you've found your brood mare?'

'Brood mare? Good heavens! Do you think that's how Ingrid took my proposal? No wonder she was upset.'

He seemed so genuinely astonished, Daisy could only shake her head in disbelief.

'You come right out, almost before dawn on a Friday morning, and ask a woman if she'll have your child. How did you expect her to take it?'

He shifted as if the chair had suddenly become too small for him.

'As a bit of a joke?' he hazarded.

'Only it wasn't,' Daisy reminded him, provoking a

long drawn-out sigh and more running of fingers through the dark hair. 'Was it?'

He shook his head.

'It seemed so simple when I started to think about it. All I had to do was find a woman who wanted children and didn't find me totally repulsive, and in return I'd offer her a home, whatever help she wanted or needed, financial security, companionship—'

'Regular sex!'

He looked so startled she laughed. 'Well, you need to go a bit further than companionship to have a child.'

Was he blushing?

Surely not!

A man who blushed?

The idea intrigued her, but pursuing it might be dangerous...

'You didn't ever answer my first question—why not go the courtship, love, marriage route to children?'

'Why don't you?' he growled, turning the question back on her.

'I asked first,' she told him, and this time it was he who laughed.

Then he stood up and said, 'Fair enough, but let's grab some sustenance for ourselves before the monsters wake up.'

He headed towards the kitchen, then turned back to where Daisy was reluctantly removing her feet from the coffee-table.

'You stay there. I owe you so much for coming to my rescue, the least I can do is fix your lunch. Any preferences? Allergies? Glass of wine with lunch? Graham not only has a great cellar in the bowels of the building, but he also has a temperature-controlled wine refrigerator in the pantry.'

'A man with his priorities right,' Daisy said, 'but no to the wine.'

Julian walked away, wondering if she'd been talking about Graham when she'd mentioned priorities, or had been making fun of him, Julian, because he knew where the wine was kept.

It was a long time since anyone had made of fun of him, he thought, considering the sensation and discovering he quite liked it. Most of the women he'd dated recently took themselves so seriously! Even as a teenager, when lust had prompted dubious declarations of love to various young women, he couldn't remember much teasing.

Forget teasing, he told himself. Right now he needed to dazzle this woman with his ability to whip up a tasty lunch—heaven forbid she should go back on her agreement to help him with the twins.

A twinge of guilt tightened his chest, but only momentarily. Even though it was a mere three days, he certainly wouldn't manage the twins on his own.

No, it was up to him, Julian Austin, to cajole, bribe, feed and in any other way he could make sure Daisy Rutherford remained on hand to help him. He opened the fridge—the food one—and peered in, but his inner mind was still on Daisy.

He pictured her, lying back in the big chair, the bright pink of her top contrasting with the dark cloud of hair.

No man in her life by choice...

He wondered why, and what had happened to make her think that way.

Pulled out olives, cheese, sun-dried tomatoes, lettuce—surely there'd be ham or pastrami, some form of cold meat.

A disastrous relationship, no doubt. Well, everyone

had those. Even he, who usually planned them meticulously. And because the fall-out at the end was always so time-consuming—so distracting from his work—he'd avoided them altogether in the last year or so.

Cheese was protein, he'd forget the meat, but maybe bread. Freezer. Ha, small portions of Turkish bread—Turkish rolls? He could defrost them in the microwave.

But she was obviously intelligent, and definitely attractive—so why would a man have let her down?

He straightened, reached out to put the food he'd gathered on the bench in the middle of the kitchen, while nudging the fridge door shut with his knee. But no matter why Daisy Rutherford had given up on men, the fact remained she was available.

Not only available, but intelligent, trained in a field related to his, which meant they'd have work in common—and she wanted a baby...

They'd be spending a lot of time together over the next three days. He'd make getting to know her a priority...

'I could have prepared lunch for a battalion in the time you've been out here.'

The priority was standing in the wide arch between the kitchen and dining areas of the apartment. The pink shirt was voluminous, but the material was fine enough to see her shape beneath it. She wasn't rake thin, but neither was she overweight, though he knew women often wore big shirts to hide what they considered a less than perfect figure. Suddenly he imagined Daisy standing there, but instead of the sweet curve of waist and hips, a beautiful bulge of pregnancy beneath the vivid shirt.

The thought produced a jolt of awareness.

She wants a sperm donor, not a husband, he reminded himself.

'I was going to throw it all on a plate, then we could help ourselves. Do you want cold meat? I'm sure there's some somewhere, I just can't put my hand on it.'

She crossed the room and opened the fridge door, bending to peer inside so her white trousers revealed a pair of neatly rounded buttocks.

'Perhaps in the tray labelled cold meats?' she said, straightening up so she could point at her find.

'I'd have looked there next,' he told her, snatching the white-wrapped deli package from her. 'So, all on one plate and help ourselves?'

She nodded her agreement, busying herself at drawers and cupboards, producing knives, napkins and a couple of bread and butter plates.

'If we don't get a move on, Shaun and Ewan will be awake again, and I believe it's your turn to keep an eye on them.'

Guilt did more than twinge this time. Julian looked at her, noticing, for the first time, the unusual colour of her eyes, neither grey nor green, yet somewhere in between, a colour he couldn't name but which was distinctive enough to deserve its own appellation.

But he couldn't be distracted by strange-coloured eyes. He busied himself setting his nibbly things on a plate, unwrapping the meat and dropping it in the centre. Or by guilt, though he could make concessions!

'You've done more than enough, considering you only came up in answer to Gabi's cry for help. I'll certainly take over for the rest of the day, but I thought, while we have lunch together, we could work out a plan of some kind.'

She smiled and the strange-coloured eyes sparkled, so for a moment they looked almost silver.

'Time on, time off, time out?' she said. 'My guess is you'll need every bit of help you can get, and so will your mother when she arrives to take over. I'll rally the troops—there are a number of us who are long-term tenants in the building and have known the twins since they were born. Gabi dumped me in this, so she's the first I'll roster on.'

Julian turned away to defrost the rolls, saying, as he used tongs to lift them on the plate, 'She did rather. Dump you in it, that is. I'm sorry. I hope you didn't feel you couldn't say no.'

Daisy laughed, the sound ringing through the kitchen.

'Don't overdo the anxiety,' she said. 'You knew exactly what strings to pull to get me to agree—Graham at death's door, Madeleine's anxiety. The only thing you left out was the fact that your father owns the building and could evict me if I didn't toe the line.'

'I'm shocked you could even think such a thing,' Julian told her, then, because he was enjoying the teasing camaraderie between them, he poked her with a well-wrapped wedge of Brie and added, 'But I'll certainly keep it in mind if you get out of hand.'

Daisy felt the contact and told herself it was only a piece of cheese, but she'd started, and knew he knew it.

Would he wonder why?

At least he didn't ask, intent on unwrapping the cheese, setting it in the last remaining space on the big plate.

'Shall we return to the living room? Those armchairs are the most comfortable seats in the house. Madeleine's dining room might look classy, but her elegant chairs are hell on a tall man's back, while my feet invariably get wedged under the curly table legs.'

Without waiting for her reply, he carried the plate into the living room. Daisy followed, thinking what a nice back he had, then realising she was probably only thinking that because it had been so long since she'd actually studied a man's back.

Not that she was studying Julian Austin's back, but as it was there, right in front of her, she could hardly miss it.

He set the food on the coffee-table—no putting her feet up now—and, taking the things she was carrying from her hands, he waved her to her chair.

'At least let me serve you,' he said, setting a piece of bread on the smaller plate and adding a selection of delicacies. 'Maybe forks?'

He looked at her, eyebrows rising as he asked the question, his eyes smiling as if to say to say, Isn't this fun?

'I can use my fingers,' she told him, and reminded herself that men couldn't be trusted, no matter how smily their eyes were. 'Do you know the children's routine, or did Madeleine leave any notes for times when you might be in charge?' she asked, to divert things back to the child-care business.

He set down his own plate, now piled with food. 'She did give me a folder—it's in my bedroom. I didn't bother reading it because Ingrid wasn't due for time off for a week and I thought by then I should know the routine.'

He smiled at her.

'Perhaps I'd better get it. Don't go away.'

He moved away then turned back to smile at her again.

'We say that so flippantly, don't we—"don't go away"? But, believe me, Daisy, this time I mean it. It's the most serious "don't go away" you're ever likely to hear. You saved my sanity by coming up this morning, and then reminding me I had a mother to come to the rescue, but who knows—maybe I'd crack completely if you disappeared before we've made our plans.'

'*Our* plans?'

'OK, my plan. The "continuing to save Julian's sanity over the weekend" plan. Is that better?'

The smile that seemed to be almost always on his lips widened appealingly, and Daisy found herself smiling back.

'I don't know why you feel you need a child to give you authenticity with the parents of your patients,' she grumbled as she waved him away. 'I would have thought you'd charm them into believing every word you uttered, whether you had personal experience or not.'

The smile flashed more brightly. 'It's a gift,' he said—no false modesty as he admitted to this ability. 'My mother said I could do it in the cradle. She thought I might have been given it in compensation for being too intelligent. Said it made people think I was human. Actually, I think, in fact, it's all to do with having far too big a mouth so I always look as if I'm smiling.'

He stopped abruptly, as if afraid he'd revealed too much to her, then said, 'I'll get the notes,' and disappeared from view.

Compensation for being too intelligent? Did he feel set apart—maybe isolated—because of his intelligence? Had it ruined relationships for him in the past?

That might explain the mutually agreed marital arrangement he had in mind—a rational business decision rather than an emotional one.

'I've got it, and guess what?'

He returned before Daisy could pursue her thoughts.

'Friday nights—I think today is still Friday—someone called Jason comes at eight, after the twins are in bed—seven o'clock bedtime is listed earlier—and minds them while we go down to dinner at Mickey's. That's the restaurant downstairs, isn't it?'

'Jason's a teenager who lives with his uncle on the third floor,' Daisy explained, 'but it can't possibly say "*we*" go down to Mickey's for dinner, because Madeleine didn't know there'd be a "we". I mean, it was always one of Ingrid's nights off, so—'

Julian's upraised hand stopped the flow.

'She meant her and Graham,' he explained, 'but she suggests I keep up the arrangement because she's paid Jason.' He glanced up and flashed one of his 'gift' smiles at Daisy.

'It might be a good idea, especially if you want to co-opt a few helpers for your mother,' Daisy agreed, breaking off a piece of bread and spreading cheese on it then adding a slice of tomato. 'You can meet some of the other tenants. Just about anyone who's off duty has either a drink or dinner in Mickey's bar on Friday nights.'

'If *I* want to co-opt?' he said in tones of such disbelief she had to hide a smile. 'What happened to teamwork? To both of us, working together? And who'll introduce me to all these strangers—?'

'Not to mention keep you safe from predatory women,' Daisy finished for him. It was no good trying not to give in to his charm—he was just too nice. 'I'll come with you,' she agreed, 'but I'll have to do some work first. So, how about I finish lunch then shoot off home, and I'll come back to help you with their dinner—does Madeleine say what time?'

Julian opened the file.

'"Five-thirty—list on fridge",' he read out.

'That's the food preference list. I saw it there earlier,' Daisy said. 'I'll be back by five—no, wait a minute, are baths before or after dinner?'

'After, surely, if they make as much mess as they did at morning tea and lunch.'

He studied the notes again.

'You're right—before.'

Horror-stricken eyes lifted to hers.

'Don't overdo it,' she told him. 'I'll come back at four-thirty.'

He read more of Madeleine's notes, as they ate, sharing titbits of information, then decided Daisy had better read them herself.

'Not right now,' she said as she finished what was on her plate. 'I really have to go.'

He didn't argue, but put down his plate and stood up, going ahead of her to open the front door and summon the lift.

'"Thank you" is a grossly inadequate phrase but I can't find a better expression,' he said, and she knew from the look in his eyes that he meant it.

'It'll do for now,' she told him, as the lift doors slid open. 'Good luck!'

The last thing she saw as the doors closed was his smile and a raised hand with his fingers waggling—like a child waving goodbye!

Part of the charm, Daisy reminded herself. Little-boy-lost impression.

But it hadn't worked on her—she'd offered to help out because her help was needed, not for any other reason. And if she found Julian Austin easy to talk to—and laugh with—it was a bonus, not a reason for minding the twins.

Down in her flat, she switched on her computer, then, while it booted up and got itself ready for work, she made herself a cup of green tea to sip while she checked her emails.

Back at her desk, she went straight to her web-page. One appeal for the guide to changing your child's eating habits which she'd put out in a newsletter a month ago. She sent off a copy to the desperate parent.

A couple of queries about ages and stages—'My two-year-old is speaking in full sentences, is he advanced?'

Aware she had to be careful answering these questions, she covered herself with the bland 'every child is different' statement, then gave what were accepted as 'normal' parameters of development.

'But we get "normal" from testing a huge number of children, then averaging them out, so there's a big difference either side of this scale which would still be considered "normal".'

She typed in the advice, then reworded sentences so she didn't have quite as much repetition. She prided herself on being able to put technical information into a form parents could understand, and had always assumed it was why her talk-back shows and web-page were popular. But sometimes it was difficult.

Yet these letters were the easy ones. The difficult ones were from parents whose children were ill or disabled, seeking some way to handle their own emotions as well as those of their children.

Daisy sighed then comforted herself with the fact that there were none like that today.

CHAPTER THREE

JULIAN tidied away the lunch dishes, checked the twins were still sleeping, then read through the rest of Madeleine's notes. He'd give them to Daisy to read—had her parents had no idea of how she'd look that they'd named her Daisy? Surely they'd have expected her to bear some genetic likeness to one or other of them—expected she might be dark-haired?

Maybe there were dark daisies he didn't know about—not just the white and golden ones the word conjured up in his mind. But they were bright and functional flowers—happy enough but everyday kind of blooms—whereas Daisy was exotic, more like an orchid.

Not that anyone in his or her right mind would call a child Orchid...

Fortunately, just as he realised how far his mind had wandered, and how absurd his train of thought was, a loud yell from the boys' bedroom suggested at least one of them was not only awake but intent on waking his brother.

Back into the fray.

Daisy, heading dutifully back up to the penthouse at four twenty-nine, met Julian in the lift, the two boys strapped into their twin stroller, quiet by virtue of the ice creams they were both eating and spreading over their skin and clothes.

'Madeleine's notes didn't mention they changed character during their afternoon sleep,' Julian growled at her, and for the first time she couldn't find any hint of a smile on his face. 'Take my advice, if you happen to be here on your own any afternoon, keep them awake. I've always recommended to parents that children need at least a rest in the afternoon, but these two? They wake up like monsters.'

'I wake up cranky if I sleep in the daytime,' Daisy told him, taking the twins straight through to the bathroom. 'They might be the same.'

'Cranky doesn't begin to cover it,' Julian told her, stripping the small, sticky bodies while she filled the tub. 'I can understand why parents get so upset with my pontificating that they demand to know if I have children of my own. It's certainly much easier in theory.'

He lifted first one little boy, then the other into the tub and stood up, apparently prepared to let Daisy do the rest.

Daisy removed the boat Ewan was using to create great splashes by slapping it down into the water, then grabbed Shaun's shoulder as he slid back and forth to create a tidal wave that was in danger of slopping over the end of the bath.

'Are you going to continue standing there watching me get wet, or do something useful like starting on their dinner?' She sneaked a quick look at the man in the doorway. 'You *can* cook, I presume?'

'Naturally!' His tone was all lofty indignation. 'In fact, I'm considered something of expert.' He paused for a moment, before adding, 'And you don't look so bad all wet.'

Daisy decided to ignore the last bit, and stick with the 'expert cook' remark.

'An expert in children's meals—a little meat and three veg?'

She turned towards him again and was rewarded with a smile.

'Basic stuff!' he scoffed, then hesitated. 'Sure you don't want a hand to lift them out and dry and dress them? That seems like a two-man job to me.'

Daisy returned the smile.

'I'll give it a go. After all, if I were to have twins, I'd be the only man available.'

He chuckled, and departed, taking with him the tension she hadn't realised had gathered in her shoulders.

By the time she reappeared with the two sweet-smelling and pyjama-clad boys, he had tea ready for them, set at a small table in the kitchen.

'We might be able to manage this,' he said, obviously pleased they'd got through the day.

'They're not in bed yet,' Daisy reminded them. 'And remember how we felt at lunchtime! We *might* be able to manage over the weekend, but I think your mother will need any assistance she can get during the week. I start part-time work on Monday but can pop up every afternoon to help her with their baths. Gabi's only working part time and I know she'll help out. She's pregnant and needs the practice. And both Alana and Kirsten will lend a hand when they can—you'll probably meet them tonight, but if they're not at Mickey's I'll talk to them tomorrow or Sunday. We usually bump into each other at breakfast in a café up the road on Sunday mornings—not by arrangement, just by being there.'

'Like Mickey's on a Friday night? Can't you have too much togetherness? Doesn't it all get a bit cloying at times?'

Daisy was startled by his questions—which were more the question of a loner than the gregarious man his smile suggested he'd be.

Though a gregarious man wouldn't be looking for an arranged marriage, would he?

Was the smile a front—a mask he wore to stop people looking past its geniality?

And if so, why?

She smiled to herself, knowing this urge to dig behind people's façades was a bad habit—probably developed from her psych studies.

'Apparently not, if that smile is anything to go by.'

His words made her realise she hadn't answered—too lost in her thoughts.

'There are a number of us who've lived in the Near West apartment building for years. I'm the newest of the group, but I've been here a couple of years,' she explained, 'so naturally friendships have developed, especially as we've all worked at Royal Westside at some time. Will you be doing consultancy work there?'

He shook his head.

'Though I'll be seeing newborns—a friend I worked with when I first went to the UK is an obstetrician at Royal Westside, and he's offered to refer to me. And I'll be visiting my own patients if that's where they happen to be admitted, but nothing else has been arranged. I've been doing hospital work and lecturing for the last few years, but I'm shifting into private practice—taking over Dr Clement's paediatric practice. Do you know him?'

He'd turned away to retrieve the spoon Ewan had flung to the floor, so wouldn't have seen Daisy's start as shock stiffened her muscles.

'Dr Clement? You're taking over from Dr Clement? On Monday?'

He might not have seen her surprise, but he certainly

heard it, for he turned to her, a puzzled frown knitting the dark eyebrows closer.

'Why? Is there something wrong with that? Something wrong with the practice? I saw the books, went into quite a lot of detail—'

'No!' Daisy managed to gulp. 'No, he's fine and it's a great practice. It's just...'

She couldn't continue, simply stared at the man she'd met only this morning but who was now, incredibly, about to become her boss.

'It's just...'

She shook her head, trying to banish disbelief, but before she had to answer, Shaun tipped over his milk and, while Julian cleaned up the mess, she took the little boy through to his bedroom to change his clothes.

'The milk will go all smelly if I don't wash it straight out,' she told Julian, when she brought Shaun back to finish his meal. 'I'll put all their soiled clothes into the machine.'

He nodded and she thought she was safe, but when she returned to the alcove off the kitchen, where the washing machine and dryer were tucked into a large cupboard, he didn't hesitate to remind her of their interrupted conversation.

'Dr Clement?'

She'd recovered enough to grin at him.

'Serendipity?' she suggested. 'I start work there Monday as well.'

'You do?'

'There's no need to sound so incredulous,' she grumbled as she checked the labels on the small garments to make sure they could all be machine-washed. 'I worked with Dr Clement years ago—for quite a while actually—doing counselling work with some of his patients. He sees a lot of children with disabilities and I provided on-site support for the parents.'

Her grouchiness vanished as she remembered.

'In fact, that was probably the most rewarding work I've ever done,' she told him, flashing him a smile that reflected the satisfaction her work had given her.

'Then why did you leave?'

Julian saw the change—it was in the darkening of her eyes, from silver to a stormcloud grey, and in the way her soft lips tightened, almost, but not quite, imperceptibly.

Yet all she did was square her shoulders, meet his eyes, and say, 'Other worlds to conquer, I guess.'

'And now?' he persisted, wanting to know more about this woman who'd so fortuitously crossed his path, a woman who wanted a baby—who was already planning to have one. Forget her silly notion of single parenthood, he'd soon talk her out of that. This was obviously meant to be.

He felt a quiver of excitement move across his skin as the physical side of him acknowledged that making babies with Daisy Rutherford, given the practice it would doubtless require, wasn't all that repulsive an idea.

The cloud-grey eyes beamed suspicion his way.

'The same answer, really. The challenge of a new adventure. Working for Dr Clement isn't new, but it's only a six-month job—filling in for a woman on maternity leave, as it happens. And after that, the baby…'

'Is that how you see having a child? As an adventure?'

The clouds vanished, blown away by a smile so natural, and heartfelt, and full of joy, he wondered if she'd smiled before her parents had named her Daisy, because it was a sunshiny, golden daisy kind of smile.

'But isn't it?' she asked. 'New discoveries every single day—new delights.'

'Wait till you take the twins to the park,' he warned, 'before you talk about delights.'

'Ho!' she responded with such abundant cheer he couldn't help but smile back at her. 'Difficulties are part of any adventure. You don't get the same joy out of your achievement if you don't have to do the hard bits.' She nodded towards the children, who were now splashing yoghurt at each other. 'And I *have* taken them to park—or minded them there while Ingrid dashed off on some mysterious errand.'

She flashed a cheeky smile at him. 'Probably booking her plane ticket to Japan.'

Julian nodded, but he was thinking about the smile—and Daisy's talk of the 'adventure' of bringing up a child.

It was a wonderful attitude, and though he hadn't considered it that way before she'd brought it up, now that he did, he agreed.

But just as his mind was floating off to a fabulous future, with a child, and a wife who was also a business partner—now, that was a coincidence too incredible to ignore—a loud yell from Ewan rudely reminded him of his responsibilities.

'I think it's bedtime,' Daisy said, crossing the room to lift Shaun from his chair. 'I'll clean this one up and get him ready.'

'You're really very good to be helping out like this,' he told her, smiling because the idea of the fabulous future hadn't entirely disappeared.

Daisy caught the smile—one of his very best. Then regretted seeing it as, to her astonishment, it made bits of her go gooey deep inside—a reaction that had been reserved, in recent times, for when she was holding newborn babies.

Was it all the talk of babies that had caused it?

She hoped so, because he smiled so often that if it kept on happening, it would make working with him very difficult.

Her being gooey inside and all...

Julian followed her into the bedroom, carrying Ewan so effortlessly that some deep primordial instinct left over from early mate-selection processes gave him full marks for his strength and caused a skitter of excitement in her autonomic nervous system.

'Thank heavens we've learnt to think and reason,' she muttered, more to herself than anyone.

'Tink and 'eason,' Shaun repeated obligingly, then his hands cupped Daisy's chin and he turned her face towards his. 'Why?'

Julian's 'Just what I wanted to ask, young man' told Daisy he, too, had heard.

'Because surely other forms of mate selection are dangerous,' she said, rubbing noses with Shaun so he'd forget he'd asked a question.

'Were we discussing mate selection?' Julian asked, and she didn't have to see his face to know his smile would be lurking.

'I was—in my head,' Daisy admitted, then wondered why herself. A number of 'whys', in fact. Why she kept answering the questions he asked. Why she didn't just shut up. Why she seemed determined to commit conversational suicide with this man.

'And do I rate a mention in this discussion?'

'Only insofar as it's all your fault,' Daisy told him, ignoring her own advice to keep quiet. 'You got us into all this trouble because of it, if you remember. Even discounting love as an ingredient for marriage, surely you must put some weight on mate selection when it comes to having a child.'

'Ah, the great adventure,' he said softly. 'Perhaps we can discuss it later, but for now let's get these imps cleaned up and ready for bed.'

She followed him into the bathroom, helped Shaun—who wanted to do it all himself—brush his teeth, then carried him through to the bedroom, feeling his tiredness in the heavy way he slumped against her.

'No unison stories tonight,' she said, when the boys were both in bed. 'I'll whip downstairs to get changed for dinner. I'll be back in time to introduce you to Jason.'

And to Alana and Rory, as it turned out.

'Oh, you've already got Daisy looking after you,' Alana said to Julian. 'Rory and I came up to ask you to join us for dinner. You still can, of course.'

Alana, newly engaged and radiating happiness, chatted on, explaining they'd also felt they should check him out for Jason's sake.

'In case you looked like an axe murderer,' Rory said, straight-faced but obviously sharing a joke with his fiancée, who dug him in the ribs.

'As if!' she said. 'You know Madeleine hates the sight of blood.'

Daisy noticed Jason watching this teasing byplay with a smile of satisfaction on his face. Rory's nephew, he was credited with bringing the two of them together, and he seemed mightily pleased with the result.

Julian was talking to him now, checking he had Mickey's number, telling the teenager to phone if he had the slightest concern.

'I'll be right,' Jason told him, 'but if you're worried, I won't lose it if you come up and check. Madeleine usually does. I think she tells Graham she's going to the ladies. He must wonder what takes her so long.'

The lad grinned at Julian, then, as if noticing Daisy for the first time, included her in his smile.

'You're looking neat,' he said. 'I'm not used to seeing you in real clothes.'

The tips of his ears went pink and he hastily amended the statement.

'Dressed up—going-out clothes—you know what I mean.'

'Of course I do, Jason, and thanks for the compliment. I'm glad your "neat" is a bit different to the one my mother used to use. Just about her favourite saying was, "For heaven's sake, girl, you can't help it if you're not pretty, but you could at least be neat." I think it was the hair that got to her. Try getting hair like this anywhere close to my mother's version of neat.'

Jason gave her a playful punch in the upper arm, and excused himself.

'The Frosts have cable TV—coming here and getting to watch it is the highlight of his week,' Rory explained, and Alana chuckled.

'No,' she said gently. 'The real highlight is if Ingrid comes home early from wherever she's been.'

Apparently she didn't notice the silence that greeted this remark, for she added, with her usual good cheer, 'Are we all ready? Daisy, are you joining us?'

Daisy grinned at her.

'Try and stop me! I mean to use the evening for a recruitment drive. And Jason's doomed to disappointment as far as Ingrid's concerned.' They all called goodnight to Jason and shuffled through the door. 'For ever,' she added as they sorted themselves into the lift.

'What do you mean?' Alana asked, but the lift had stopped again, the doors opening to reveal Kirsten Collins and her soon-to-be husband, Josh Phillips.

More introductions, so, as Josh and Julian were playing the 'do you know so-and-so' game of fellow paediatricians, Daisy didn't have a chance to answer Alana's question.

But as they walked across the ground-floor foyer and into Mickey's, Kirsten turned to her and asked, 'Did Ingrid leave? Do you know?'

Though she should, by now, be used to Kirsten knowing just about everything that went on in the building, Daisy was still startled.

'Did you see Gabi? Did she tell you?' Daisy demanded.

Kirsten shook her head.

'Ingrid told me—just days before the Frosts left—and I had the most dreadful time trying to decide if I should tell Madeleine, but I was sure if I did she'd put off the trip, and Graham's been so sick they both needed the break. Then, on top of that, I knew Madeleine's brother would be here, and who better than a paediatrician to mind the twins?'

'Would you let Josh do it?' Daisy asked, and saw Kirsten's blithe confidence fade.

'Well, probably not!' she said doubtfully. 'I mean, he might know kids as patients, but he doesn't know that many personally. Except his brothers' children and they don't behave like kids. I think they were born perfect little Phillips clones. It positively terrifies me to think I might either produce more of the same, or perhaps be expected to. I'm not sure which option is worse.'

Daisy chuckled, but as the rest of the party had already gone into Mickey's and Julian was holding the door open for the two laggards, she gave Kirsten a reassuring pat on the shoulder and urged her forward.

Not that she went far. No sooner were they through the door, and Julian had gone ahead to join the others at the bar, than Kirsten stopped again.

'So what's going to happen? Is Julian getting someone to come in—an emergency nanny of some kind?'

'What are you two whispering about?' Alana turned back to join them. 'Is it to do with the recruitment drive you mentioned?'

So Daisy explained, carefully omitting the excuse Ingrid had given for her tantrum and detouring around any mention of babies, other than the twins.

'I can see Julian's point about keeping it from Madeleine, but his mother will definitely need help,' Alana said. 'That pair are a handful.'

'Yes,' Daisy agreed, perhaps a little too wholeheartedly, 'But I'll only be working part time, so I can pop up most afternoons.'

'You're too good to be true, Daisy,' Kirsten said, shaking her head in mock-disbelief. 'How did you get into it anyway? Did you know the hunky Julian?'

'Hunky?' Daisy echoed. 'Do you think he's hunky?'

Kirsten laughed and shook her head.

'You can't tell me you didn't notice the hunkiness,' she said, then frowned severely at Daisy. 'Honestly, I'm seriously worried about you. Take a good look at the man and tell me what you see.'

She turned Daisy so she was facing the bar, where the three men were chatting easily.

'He's big,' Daisy said. 'I noticed that straight away.

And, though I can't see it right now, he's got a nice smile.'

Kirsten shook her head again.

'I give up,' she said to Alana. 'Here she's spent the entire day with a man who puts our not-bad-looking blokes in the shade as far as handsome is concerned, and all she's noticed is that he's big and has a nice smile.'

'And lovely eyes,' Daisy added belatedly, desperate to make up for the lack of admiration her friends found so unbelievable.

'Come on,' Alana said, putting an arm around her shoulder and urging her forward. 'We should know by now that Daisy inhabits a parallel universe. She sees far too much we'd just as soon she didn't see—about us, I mean—and completely misses stuff we take for granted.'

She planted a kiss on her friend's cheek.

'But we love you anyway,' she assured her, giving her a quick hug before releasing her.

But far from being reassured, Daisy was left seriously worried. It was OK for *her* to wonder if maybe she'd slipped into a parallel universe, but for her friends to be seeing her that way...

It was a pleasant evening, so much so that Daisy wondered if she'd been missing a normal social life more than she'd realised.

'How about a nightcap in the penthouse?' Julian suggested, and though the others all agreed, the men anxious to see Graham's new wine fridge which had been a major topic of conversation during the evening, Daisy declined.

'If I'm giving you a hand with the twins tomorrow, I'll need an early night.' It was true, but it still sounded like an excuse, and from the way Julian looked at her, he'd read it that way as well.

Which was possibly why, when she answered a knock on her door at eight the next morning, he was standing there.

Looking anxious.

'You *are* up!' he said, shifting as if his weight was too much for his feet to bear. 'I was in a bind—not wanting to wake you but wanting you to know you could sleep in if you wanted to, which, of course, you couldn't if I knocked on the door and woke you. The angel Gabi came knocking on my door just after the others had left, to say she and Alex would take the twins today. I got them up and fed them, and she's just whisked them off, in Madeleine's car so they're in their own car-seats, for a day at the beach.'

There was a pause, and he shifted again.

'Why don't you come in and sit down?' said Daisy. 'I was making pikelets for the twins but I can turn them into pancakes and we can have them as breakfast—or brunch if you breakfasted with the twins.'

Julian stepped cautiously through the door.

Yesterday, in vivid pink, Daisy had looked exotic, but today's shirt, again loose-fitting and in a fine material, was a deep purple, so again she stood out like an exotic bloom, especially as the comfortably furnished living room was homely and welcoming—but definitely unexotic.

He sat, because she'd suggested it, then felt foolish as she'd returned to the kitchen, presumably to turn pikelets into pancakes. He could see her head and shoulders above the breakfast bar dividing the kitchen off from the living and dining space.

'You don't *have* to sit,' she called to him, divining

his thoughts so correctly he took it as a sign that all the things he'd been thinking weren't so impossible after all.

Thus armoured with conviction, he stood up and walked towards her, propping himself against the bar and folding his arms.

Daisy was pouring the thinned batter into a shallow pan, swirling the pan so it spread, and the conviction that this woman was perfect for what he had in mind—a sensible, rational, non-emotional marriage—grew.

'It's fantastic really—Gabi taking the twins—because it will give us a chance to get to know each other better.'

She turned, flipped the pancake with a quick flick of her wrist, then frowned ferociously at it before turning back to him.

'Fantastic?'

'Yes. Don't you see how everything's falling into place? First we meet like we did, then I find you're going to be working with me.' He paused, then asked, 'The other psychologist? The one you're replacing. Is she definitely coming back or just saying she will to get maternity leave?'

He watched as Daisy took a plate out of a warming oven, slid the pancake on to it, returned the plate to where it had been and poured more mixture into the pan, before turning back to him.

'Is your cynicism showing, Doctor?'

He grinned at her.

'You must admit, people do that kind of thing.'

Daisy might have agreed but she wasn't admitting anything. Another pancake was removed from the pan, the process carrying on without the slightest hitch though it was obvious from her smile that her attention wasn't on the job.

Encouraged by the smile, Julian continued. 'I wondered because I was thinking how convenient it would be if you stayed on in the job. Convenient for you, me and the baby. We'd be partners in business as well as in marriage.'

He looked hopefully at her, but as she was adding a sixth pancake to the pile, she didn't answer immediately. Neither could he see her face to gauge a reaction, though when she said 'Excuse me?' in a disbelieving voice, he assumed she wasn't as struck by the idea as he was.

But when she added, 'There is no "you, me and the baby", Julian,' he thought he heard a lack of conviction in her words.

'Ah, but maybe there could be. That's what we have to discuss.'

Silence, apart from the splat of a pancake flipping back into the pan.

'Surely we won't eat more than that,' he said, when it became obvious she wasn't going to answer.

I won't eat any, the way my stomach feels at the moment, Daisy thought. Having babies, partnerships—all on offer from a man who can make my insides go gooey! This is weird stuff!

But out loud she said, 'I'm just finishing up the batter. This is the last.'

He waited until she lifted it out, then strode forward, turned off the gas, grabbed her shoulders and moved her away from the stove.

'You get out whatever you need to spread over them, I'll find cutlery and plates. I can't continue a sensible business discussion with a woman who keeps flipping pancakes. It's the most distracting thing I've ever seen. I mean, it must take a certain amount of concentration, so I know you can't be listening—'

'I did hear you,' Daisy told him, putting honey and

maple syrup on the bar, adding butter in case Julian liked that as well. 'But I've already explained that I don't want a husband, let alone a business partner. I don't need either to—'

'To have a baby,' Julian finished for her. 'But you only think that way because you haven't thought about alternatives. You haven't considered other options, probably because there wasn't a man around who might fit the bill. This is ideal, Daisy, don't you see? As partners in business as well as marriage, we can make our own rules. You can have whatever maternity leave you want, and if you want to keep working, you could bring the baby to work and we could organise some child-care, and both be there for him—or her—'

'Partners in business as well as marriage? Julian, let's get real here. You've known me less than twenty-four hours, you can't possibly want to marry me.'

He looked so startled she wondered if she'd missed a day or two—maybe a month—somewhere, and they actually had a relationship she didn't know about.

'Why ever not? I agree, we need to talk a bit more, but you wouldn't have said "Actually, I might"—see, I even remember the words—when I suggested the baby bit, if there was someone else in your life. Think about it, Daisy. You want a baby, I want a baby, we're going to be working together. If you decide to keep working part time, that would be a bonus for me, but if you don't want to work that's OK, too.'

He forked two pancakes onto her plate and pushed it towards her, but how could she think about eating?

'I'm rushing you, I know,' he continued, as if his thoughts couldn't be contained, 'but babies take so darned long to get from conception to birth and then even longer to become really useful to a paediatrician father, I feel I need to get started on the project as soon as possible.'

Daisy stared at her pancakes, noticing the nice even brown colour which would normally have filled her with satisfaction that she'd got them just right. But today they could have been scorched black for all she cared. In fact, it was a wonder they weren't, so distracted had she been, not only by Julian's presence in her kitchen—any man's presence in her kitchen—but by the weird conversation.

The latest revelation—his assumption that all this was possible—had simply been the last shock in a number of shocks—and one too many for her to contemplate.

Fortunately, he didn't seem to be similarly discomposed, for he continued talking as if their conversation were about something as basic as the weather.

'Tell me why *you* want a baby and why you're not going the conventional meeting, courtship, relationship route?'

Immensely cheered to get something she *could* answer, Daisy poured syrup onto her pancakes, then cut across the top so the sweet liquid would ooze down between them.

'I've always wanted children, and…'

Perhaps it wasn't such an easy question after all.

'And?'

The word hung in the air and, without looking at him, she could hear the smile in it.

She half smiled herself.

'Do you know a song from an old musical about a cock-eyed optimist? I guess that's what I was. My parents had a terrible relationship. They parted when I was six, and since then my mother's gone from man to man—I think there's an old song about that, too—which should have made me very cynical, but did it? No way.

I went into every relationship I ever had—which isn't many as I finally saw the light—thinking this is it, and hearing wedding bells and the chatter of small children.'

'Really?'

He sounded so astonished she stopped playing with her pancakes and turned towards him. He *looked* astonished, too. Not even smiling.

'Is there something wrong with that?' she demanded. 'With believing in love?'

He shook his head and took up a forkful of pancake—probably so he didn't have to answer—chewed, swallowed...then smiled.

'Nothing at all,' he assured her, still smiling but in such a way she knew he meant it. 'Nothing at all. Especially if you're young. The thing people label love is a very powerful emotion in youth, though less life-altering as one grows older. Do you know, statistically speaking—?'

He broke off and offered her another smile—this one apologetic. 'Sorry. I've spent a lot of time in university confines where theory reigns supreme.'

By this time, Daisy had no idea what they'd been talking about when she'd taken up the cudgels in defence of love.

Fortunately, Julian seemed to have remained on track, for he asked, 'So, what's happened to you—a believer in love—that you're giving love a miss and going for a baby along a less conventional path?'

'I found out it didn't work for me. I still believe in it,' she added sturdily, 'but I've finally figured out—it might be genetic, given my mother's behaviour—that the love route isn't for me. It's my own fault. I think I love too hard and turn the loved one off, though I tend to have abominable taste in men as well. Three out of three, all following exactly the same pattern of meeting, attraction, lust—you can't discount that in relationships, in fact it's probably where a lot of them go wrong—then, bingo, just when I think I can get the invitations printed, the guy departs from my life, usually in some spectacular fashion.'

She paused for a moment then said thoughtfully, 'Actually, I could probably go on one of those programmes you sometimes see on daytime television. American programmes where the behind-the-scenes teams gather a group of people who all have weird love lives for the front person to interview. You know. Today's guests "have all married their girlfriend's mother's husband's baby" or "had sex with their uncle's publican"—you know the kind of thing.'

Julian laughed, then pointed his finger at her.

'I refuse to believe it can be that bad.'

'Believe!' she said, and nodded seriously. 'Even in between the main three, there were losers. One guy I was asked to run a psych test on for a court case—a simple break-and-enter case but he was pleading diminished responsibility for some reason. He was good-looking and fun, and he asked me out. Of course, I went, stupid romantic fancies of curing him of his wicked ways floating freely in my head, and what happens but he somehow made a copy of my flat key—he'd never even been to my flat, I'm not totally stupid—let himself in and stole all my electrical equipment.'

'You know it was him?' Julian said in the kind of awed voice usually reserved for 'stranger than fiction' stories.

Daisy grinned at him.

'He hadn't done all that well on his IQ score, you know,' she admitted, 'so, of course, he left fingerprints all over the place. Apparently one of the reasons he was in court was for ripping off his girlfriends, but because he'd often been living in their flats, his fingerprints weren't considered evidence. He kind of forgot he hadn't been in mine.'

Julian shook his head.

'After that story, I hardly like to ask about the ones you call the "main" ones.'

'Actually, the first, Peter, wasn't too bad. He just got uppity and left. He hadn't minded me doing better than him in exams when we were both in high school, blaming that on girls maturing faster than boys, but when I started getting higher marks than him in university subjects—which we'd studied for together—he did a big dummy spit and that was that.'

'So the first potential father proved a flop. What happened next?'

Daisy stared at him, unable to answer because his phrasing had startled her.

'Do you think that's what I've been doing? Thinking so far ahead—to the babies—I've only considered the men as father material? Because I didn't have a father, perhaps? Well, not one I knew very well.'

She frowned at Julian, and he smiled and shook his head. 'Lady, you're the psychologist, but don't over-analyse this. You are, no doubt, perfectly normal, and went into your relationship with the weakling who couldn't hack you being brighter than him for all the usual reasons—attraction, liking, lust—you mentioned. Tell me about number two.'

'I took a while to get to number two. I went out with a few men a few times and nothing happened—no magic, no desire to take things further. Then Adrian came along and the "this is it" syndrome kicked in again. Except eventually it turned out he was gay and I was an experiment,' Daisy said, cheerful again because she knew she hadn't lost Adrian because of who or what she was. 'He thought a relationship with a woman would "cure" him, but I didn't have a clue about that, of course, and he was so gorgeous—'

'Perfect father material?' Julian murmured, and Daisy rounded on him.

'I *wasn't* looking for a father for my children. I wanted a relationship—I fell in love. Children were a long way down the track, particularly as Adrian was a struggling artist.'

She hesitated then added, 'Though recently I have considered him a possible sperm donor. When I decided to have a child.'

'And number three—you did say three.'

Daisy felt the customary jolt of pain that wasn't so much loss of love as betrayal.

'Glen!' The name slipped out before it could stop it, but she pulled herself together to add, 'I don't talk about number three.' She hoped she sounded ultra-calm, though her fingers were shaking so much she put down her knife and fork in case Julian noticed.

'But he's definitely not a candidate?'

'Definitely not.'

'Not likely to make a come-back, like some aging sports or rock star?'

'No!'

He was pushing her and she snapped the word at him, but, rather than take offence, he seemed pleased, for he smiled as he used the last remaining pancake to mop what was left of the syrup from his plate.

'So that leaves the field free for me,' he said, and she wasn't sure if the satisfaction she heard in his voice was from the breakfast or the conversation. 'That's if we discount Adrian, which I think we should, don't you? There are all kinds of complications that could arise from having a donor, you know.'

'But I'd know you,' Daisy said, aware she was back in the other world again but quite enjoying the bizarreness of the conversations in it.

'But I won't be a donor who does the deed then disappears. I'd be in it for the long haul. That's what I'm trying to tell you. I'm not saying I'll be a perfect father, but I'd be a hands-on one. I know I talk about having a baby for professional reasons, but I love kids and really do want one or two of my own, for the same reasons you want one. I'd be there for you as well, partners, whatever the world might throw at us.'

And suddenly, whatever universe she might currently be inhabiting, the idea of having a partner seemed very appealing. To have someone there for *her*. She peered suspiciously at Julian. Had he phrased it that way because he guessed just how badly she'd always wanted that kind of security? How unloved—unlovable—she'd always felt, that she thrown herself into relationships with such gusto?

But how could he have guessed? None of her friends saw that neediness in her. In fact, they tended to think her happily self-contained and envied her complacence.

She stared at Julian, and saw what Alana and Kirsten had seen immediately.

A very good-looking man.

'Why are you doing this?' she asked. 'Let's forget me and talk about you for a change. Why is a man who has a good career, and the potential to earn a decent income, and looks and charm, planning a marriage of convenience—because that's what it is to you, isn't it?'

'Because I want a child,' he repeated, but she knew there was more. Partly because his smile had disappeared and that rarely happened, and partly because his eyes had darkened to a deep, fathomless green.

She didn't react, didn't speak—just waited. It was an old psychologist's trick and she knew he probably knew it, but she also knew that most people eventually had to break a silence.

'I went into medicine from a science background, Daisy, so I'm sceptical when it comes to romantic love. I mean, it's not a concept that can be measured or proven, is it?' he said, when she'd all but decided he was the exception.

'When we're young we have urges and enthusiasms we label love. It even happened to me a few times—typical young male stereotype. A young girl who looks spectacular comes into one's orbit, testosterone kicks in, youth flings himself at her feet, spouting all the stuff you hear in pop songs and read in magazines. But it gets messy, Daisy. As far as I can make out, the depth of feelings between the two always differs—you said yourself you suspected you loved too hard. It's like a seesaw, and without balance it can tip suddenly and one or other of the couple either slide off or is flung up into the air.'

Daisy heard the words, devoid of emotion, and understood he'd given it serious thought, though she suspected some woman in the past had let him down for him to have analysed love so thoroughly and discarded it as an option in his life. The knowledge caused a heaviness in her chest and a niggling sense of disappointment, but whether for Julian or herself she wasn't certain.

He took her chin and, as Shaun had the previous evening, turned her face so he could look into her eyes.

'Things happen when we're young, our libidos on the rampage. At that time of one's life all the emotions are exaggerated, but, fortunately, as we get older, that kind of heat dies. You and I are mature, intelligent adults, and there's no reason why we shouldn't make a go of things—if you're willing to give it a try. You called it a marriage of convenience, as if there was something wrong with that idea, but it's a system which worked for our forebears for generations—and it still happens in a lot of countries and cultures. Statistically, arranged marriages work better than so-called love matches. If you consider the divorce rate today, perhaps it might be a more sensible approach to marriage.'

Daisy met his gaze, the hazel eyes gleaming with what looked like excitement. But she was still in a state of shock. If raising children was a great adventure, how did going into marriage with a stranger rate?

'We mightn't like each other—I mean, when we actually get to know each other better. And we mightn't be sexually compatible.'

He leant forward and brushed his lips across hers.

'To answer the last objection first, I think sexual compatibility is something you learn, not something that happens through any imagined emotional joining. As for the liking—we don't have to get married tomorrow, but I doubt that would be a problem. It's not as if we'd be going into it with any illusions or expectations beyond a mutually satisfactory relationship.'

She frowned at him, disturbed by her reaction to the touch of his fingers on her chin, the brush of his lips against hers.

'There are conception problems, too,' she reminded

him, determined to be as practical as he was. 'It would be silly to get married unless I was pregnant, wouldn't it?'

Julian moved his fingers against the soft skin on Daisy's chin, wondering why he was still holding it but not wanting to break the physical contact.

'I guess so,' he agreed, wondering now if he'd ever considered the softness of a woman's skin—*really* considered it.

'Of course so,' Daisy said, standing up so his hand fell away. 'The whole point of the exercise is that we both end up with a child. I may be infertile, or your sperm might be incompatible with my ova. A heap of things can happen, and we'd be stuck with each other, or have to pay perfectly good money for a divorce so we could each start again.'

She was right, of course, but he didn't like the idea of starting again. The experience with Ingrid—and a couple of minor skirmishes in the past—had shown him how difficult arranged marriages were to arrange. Pure luck had thrown Daisy in his path, but it was unlikely he'd get this lucky twice.

Or get anyone as perfect as Daisy appeared, on first acquaintance, to be for a partner.

He followed her into the kitchen, stopping behind her where she was working at the sink. Reaching over her shoulder, he took the dishcloth from her hands.

'I'll do this,' he said, hoping she was as aware of his body as he was of hers. 'You relax. We've the day to ourselves so we should make the most of it—get to know each other a little better. There's a great spa in the penthouse if you feel like total relaxation a little later.'

Daisy turned, trapped between the sink and his body.

'This is mad,' she said. 'We've just met and we're—'

'We're...' he queried, knowing exactly what she was thinking.

'Moving rapidly towards going to bed together, aren't we?' she murmured, the grey-green eyes huge in her pale face.

'Not until you're ready,' he promised, but he bent his head and kissed her while his body accommodated itself to her shape and size, not pressing against her but fitting itself to hers as if only by this means could it know her.

'You *are* Madeleine's brother?' she said doubtfully, when he stopped kissing her.

'Does that help?' he teased, knowing she was talking herself into the next stage of their arrangement.

'Not really,' she admitted. 'I'm very fond of Madeleine, but I've always found her a bit...'

'Scatty?' Julian offered. 'She is, but she's got a heart of gold. Anyway, I take after my father who's a straightforward and sensible businessman.'

'Oh, I can see the sensible part,' Daisy said, and he felt her body relax slightly as her lips softened into a smile. 'Offering to make babies with two women in one day. Not at all scatty. Very sensible.'

'Wretch!' he said, and, because she'd made him smile, he kissed her again.

But this time she squirmed away.

'I should check my emails. I have an interactive web site and answer queries on it.'

She ducked under his imprisoning arm and dashed away, leaving him to wipe the dishes then move cautiously through the small flat in search of her.

The computer was set up in a corner of the bedroom, the fit so snug she had to sit on the bed to use it. The bedroom door was open so she noticed his arrival and motioned him to come in.

'You'll have to sit on the bed to see the screen, but you might as well have a look. There are a couple of queries that are fairly representative of what I get asked.'

There was no trace of coyness or embarrassment in her voice as she invited him in and he congratulated himself on finding such a practical woman—then remembered it had been pure luck, not any brilliance on his part. Hardly cause for congratulation!

'See.'

She pointed to the screen, indicating the box where the questions came through.

'"How do I know my child's got ADHD?"' he read aloud. 'Well, at least she knows about the hyperactivity component that's usually included in diagnoses these days. How do you answer?'

Daisy turned and smiled at him.

'Not with a list of the inattention behaviours or a detailed account of hyperactivity/impulsivity. If you tell parents their child needs to show six of each type of sign for a diagnosis, they immediately see those behaviours in the child and, no doubt, dutifully report them to their doctor or paediatrician.'

Julian smiled his approval, but she wasn't finished.

'Though anyone can find the lists if he or she wants to badly enough. In books, on the internet. Information's readily available these days.'

'It's the same with everything. You've no idea the number of patients I see who have already been diagnosed, usually correctly, by their parents.'

'I guess it's good,' Daisy said, tapping away at the keys so he knew only part of her attention was on their conversation. 'But at least if they come to see you, they know they need help. They're not trying to cure the child as well.'

Julian nodded his agreement—not that she'd have seen the nod—and read the words she was typing. '"It's impossible to diagnose ADD or ADHD without a proper examination and study of the child, so I suggest you take him or her to a good paediatrician…"'

'You could have given me a recommendation there,' he interrupted his reading to say, but, apart from a look shot at him across her shoulder, she ignored him and kept typing.

'"—and have the child tested properly. It's possible there's some other cause for the inattention, and the paediatrician will test hearing, eyesight, comprehension skills and a host of other things which could be causing the problem."'

'Well said,' Julian agreed, then watched as, fingers moving swiftly, Daisy cut and pasted some information on how to improve a child's attention span, and another article on physical activities which would help develop the mental side of a child's brain.

'You wrote those yourself?' he asked, as she pressed more keys and sent the lot spinning into cyber-space.

'Of course! Plagiarism's unacceptable even on the net, though I don't doubt a lot of it goes on.'

'And the second question you had in the box? The one from the grandmother who thinks her grandson is being abused by his mother's boyfriend?'

Daisy sighed and turned to face him.

'How do you answer things like that?' she said. 'What I want to do is grab the child and take him right away, to love and nurture him and keep him safe, but his mother probably loves him, too. And the grandmother might be wrong.'

She sighed again.

'I usually suggest she spends more time with the

child—perhaps offer to mind him more often so the boyfriend is under less pressure.'

'And isn't left alone with the child?'

'That, too,' Daisy said. 'And I give the number of the Children's Services Department, but that's very risky because if the grandmother makes a fuss, it could anger the daughter to such an extent she cuts all ties with her mother and so loses support when she most needs it.'

Julian heard the pain in her voice and asked quietly, 'Do you get many emails like that?'

'Not so many emails, but on talk-back radio it sometimes seemed as if every night someone was worried about a child at risk.'

'Yet you want a child of your own?' Julian said, and saw her face lighten as she smiled.

'So I can give it all the love these other mites miss out on. Sounds stupid, but sometimes it seems as if it's the only way I can make the world right again.'

Julian closed his eyes briefly and thanked the fates that had set this woman in his path. They'd led him down some false tracks occasionally, but now it seemed as if they were eager to put things right.

He reached out and took both of Daisy's hands in his, marvelling at how small they felt in his far larger ones.

'I would be honoured to be the father of that child,' he said, 'and though I said I wouldn't press you for an answer or rush you into this, we're neither of us getting any younger.'

She laughed, a sound of such sheer delight it sparked a chord deep within him, and a warmth started where for so long there'd been coldness. Companionship—he knew that's all it was, but how wonderful to feel it again.

CHAPTER FOUR

'AREN'T you going to reply to the final question?' Julian asked, as Daisy retrieved her hands, turned back to the monitor and shifted to another page of her web-site.

She didn't answer, pretending that hitting the 'forward' button took a great deal of concentration.

'The one from the young man who fancies himself in love,' he persisted, and Daisy gave in, going back to the question-and-answer page.

'I get these all the time,' she said, 'and as both the questions and the answers are there for all to read—I don't reply privately to anyone—you'd think he'd know what I think.'

She read the question again.

'Do you think love lasts?' It was signed, 'In Love'.

'You said "young man in love",' she said, turning back to Julian. 'What makes you think "In Love" is a male?'

'Males are far less committed to the concept of love, aren't they? Generally speaking, they put less value on it. They do what they can, of course, to keep a woman happy...'

'But it's more to do with sex than love?' Daisy murmured, but she was already replying.

'In my opinion, romantic love just happens. It's a mix of many things, attraction, lust and infatuation being only a few possible components. But relationships must be built, and building a solid relationship takes time, patience and understanding, also a measure of compromise—a whole lot of give and take—plus a whole heap of unselfishness and commitment. If you can build a good relationship with the person you love, then your love will most certainly last.'

'Do you believe that?' Julian asked. He'd come closer and was now leaning over her shoulder, and though she was used to friends being in the room as she replied to questions on her web-site, today Julian's closeness was making her uneasy.

'Yes,' she told him, finishing with her signature line and the smiling daisy, which had seemed cute when the web magician had drawn it in but was now beginning to irritate her.

'In spite of your own…?'

He hesitated and she finished for him, 'Disastrous relationships? Of course. Just because it didn't work for me doesn't mean it won't work for someone else. What I should have told "In Love" was that both of them had to be working on building the relationship—not just one of them.'

She must have sounded depressed or defeated because she felt Julian's hand close on her shoulder then he drew her back against him and gave her a hug. The kind of hug Adrian still gave her when they met occasionally, or Gabi's husband Alex might give her when she hadn't seen him for a while.

A friendly hug.

Only in this case she took it as a comforting one.

And tried not to think that it might also be a kind of lead-up one—that Julian might be working on the 'compatibility takes practice' issue.

'So, you're free for the day—what are you going to do?' she asked, drawing away in case it was a compatibility-practice hug. Even in parallel universes it wasn't good to move too quickly.

'What are *we* going to do? I did hope you'd take pity on a newcomer to town and spend the day with him.'

Not in the spa, Daisy said to herself, then she remembered he was Madeleine's brother.

'But you're hardly a newcomer. You grew up here in Westside, didn't you?'

'I went to primary school here, then boarding school down south in Sydney. I was bright, you see, and my parents thought it would be best. The school had an accelerated learning programme. So from school it was natural to go on to university down there, and eventually into medicine. I haven't really lived here permanently since I was ten, though I had holidays here until Mum and Dad shifted further north.'

He was smiling at her and, though she didn't want to give in, the smile won her over, especially as her heart had gone out to the clever ten-year-old sent away to boarding school. Like her, he'd missed out on a normal family life, although for different reasons.

'I guess we can do something,' she conceded. 'But I dressed in ''playing with the twins'' clothes. If we're doing the town, I need to change. What if we meet in the foyer in half an hour?'

He held his hands in the air, and pretended to look shocked.

'A woman who can be ready in half an hour?' Then, before she could defend the members of her sex, he looked down at his clothes. 'What about me? Will this do or are we going somewhere special?'

She looked him over, and though she was supposed to be checking out his clothes—he was in shorts today—she couldn't but notice the strongly muscled legs and mentally note that his physical genes were certainly very good.

'I'd like to call in at Royal Westside hospital. I realise that makes it a bit of a busman's holiday for you, but there's a child there I visit. One of Josh's patients who's just had a bone-marrow transplant. Her parents live in the Northern Territory—on one of the more remote properties up there—and though one or other of them tries to get down fortnightly, a number of friendly volunteers fill in on the other weekend.'

'I'd like to do that—it would give me a chance to see something of the hospital. But I'll shed the shorts. A lot of what we medical people do is helped by the image we project, isn't it?'

'Maybe not so much what we do, but the success of what we do,' Daisy said, wondering how she could speak so calmly when in her mind she was watching a kind of internal video of Julian Austin shedding his shorts.

Revealing far more than well-muscled legs...

'I know it shouldn't be,' she continued, averting her mind firmly from the mental images, 'but I'm sure people have more confidence in a professional if he or she looks neat and tidy. Not that I'm into power dressing, but I'll swap shorts for a skirt.'

And a very nice skirt it was, Julian decided when he met up with Daisy in the foyer a little later. Short enough to show shapely legs but not so short it would ride up and reveal underwear if she bent down to speak to a sick child. Practical! But still the vibrant colours she seemed to favour, the skirt white but splashed with pink, blue and violet flowers, while the neat blue top, tucked in sedately at the waist, made her eyes, for some unfathomable reason, look more green than grey.

'Hospital first?' he said, aware his assessment had probably gone on too long.

'I thought so, then I've booked a lunch cruise on the river. It's the best way to see the city.'

'Fabulous, but I'll pay,' he insisted, then he linked his arm through hers and they walked out into the mellow autumn sunshine.

The hospital was familiar as he'd done a month of work experience there while still a student, but the new transplant unit in the paediatrics ward was eye-opening in its brilliance.

'Most of this was Kirsten's idea,' Daisy told him, feeling as proud of her friend as a mother must of a clever child. 'She wanted some kind of stimulating visual attraction that would interest even the sickest of children, and a cousin of Josh's came up with the computer program while she organised the painting of the isolation rooms. My friend Bella is out of there now, but you can look through the windows if you want to see what I mean.'

Julian looked, and watched a little boy, with help from a woman who was probably his mother, run his fingers over a touch pad, manipulating images on the wall.

'It's unbelievable!' he marvelled. 'Boredom's such an issue with these kids, and if they're bored they don't do as well—almost as if they lose the will to fight because there's nothing in their life worth fighting for.'

'Exactly!' Daisy agreed, and although she felt a flutter of excitement that he shared her opinions, she reminded herself that most professionals would.

Professional compatibility was easy.

'This is Bella,' she said, leading him away from the special isolation rooms to a partly curtained-off alcove on one side of the open ward.

Bella was smiling and waving to her and Daisy hurried across, digging in her handbag for the new selection of farm animals she'd brought along.

'I'll never be able to get as many cattle as you have at your home,' she told the little girl, after giving the fragile body a gentle hug, 'but I found some Brahmans this time—isn't that what your dad breeds?'

She put the plastic bag of toy animals on the bed, then found scissors to cut open the top. Bella spilled the tiny models on the sheet, then looked up at Daisy and smiled.

'And I brought you a new visitor as well,' Daisy said, stepping aside so Bella could get a good look at Julian. 'His name's Julian and he's a doctor, like Dr Josh, only he doesn't work in this hospital.'

Julian put out his hand and Bella, with the trust of youth, put her tiny one into it and gravely shook hands.

'Let's show Julian how we set up the farm,' Daisy suggested, reaching down under the bed for the large piece of plywood she'd painted to represent Daisy's home—or as much of it as would fit on a hospital bed.

Bella crossed her legs to make room for the board, and reached into the drawer of her bedside cabinet to produce a brightly coloured cloth bag. From this she tipped an assortment of animals and tiny model buildings, sorting through them until she came to what she wanted.

Julian noted her pallor, the small, hairless head, the drip pushing drugs into her veins. He'd have liked to check her chart, but felt that would compromise his visitor status. Then suddenly the child, who'd set a house and several sheds in the middle of the board, asked, 'Are you a children's doctor?'

'Yes, I am,' he told her, judging her to be five or six,

though with developmental delays from drugs she could be a little older.

'Do you know about AML?' she asked, and Julian felt his heart squeeze. Though various forms of the disease had differing success rates, generally the chance of curing a child with any of the acute myeloid leukaemias was less than fifty per cent. In fact, not much more than forty per cent.

'Yes, I do. Is that your problem?'

'No,' Bella said cheerfully, 'it's Mum's problem, and Dad's too, I suppose. My problem is getting better as quickly as I can. Daisy couldn't find me a proper kelpie—that's a cattle dog—but I use this dog...' she held up a miniature collie for Julian to inspect '...and pretend it's my dog Bliss. I have to get better so I can go home and take care of him. Dr Josh gave me special treatment that made me very, very sick. I nearly died, didn't I, Daisy?'

Daisy nodded and her eyes met Julian's, the look in them confirming the child's words.

'She had an autologous bone-marrow transplant,' Daisy said quietly, and Julian visualised the procedure where, at a time when Bella had been in complete remission, a little of her own bone marrow would have been harvested and then transplanted back into her later, where, hopefully, it would rebuild healthy bone marrow. Because of the risk of affected cells still hiding in the transplanted marrow, the process was only used if no compatible donor could be found. And though the pretransplant and the recovery processes were much the same as in a marrow donation from someone else, because the child's marrow was so depleted of cells, it took far longer for an improvement to show in the blood count, which would account for the child's extreme pallor.

'But now I'm getting better and Dr Josh says I'm the one who's going to beat the odds. That's funny, isn't it? Grandma has mats she takes outside and hangs on the clothes line and she hits them with a broom and says she's beating the carpets, but what are odds and how do you beat them? With brooms?'

Julian chuckled.

'With brooms, and luck, and with a lot of tenacity and courage, which, it seems to me, you have by the bucket-load, young lady.'

'The lion in *The Wizard of Oz* was looking for some courage.'

'Well, if he happens to come here looking,' Julian told her, 'I'm sure you've got enough to spare for him.'

Bella laughed.

'Silly!' she said, shaking her head over the stupidity of adults. 'He's not real—he's in a book. No, Daisy, the cattle go over here—that paddock's for the horses.'

Dismissing Julian—no doubt because he was so silly—she turned her attention back to her farm, shifting the cattle Daisy had been carefully setting out and putting horses in their place.

'Unless it's muster or sale time we don't really see the cattle close to the house,' Bella explained, no doubt for Julian's benefit. 'They run in the gullies and the far paddocks. My dad has a helicopter to muster them. Can you fly a helicopter?'

Julian admitted he was lacking that particular skill, but proved a dab hand at setting out animals, even if he did get a tiger mixed in with the herd of cattle.

'That tiger should be in the other bag,' Bella said crossly, and Daisy, apparently understanding this remark, reached into the bedside cabinet and produced another cloth bag, this one patterned with zoo animals.

'When we turn over the board, I can make a zoo,' Bella told him. 'Daisy made the board for me. She's kind, isn't she?'

'It certainly seems so,' Julian agreed, beaming at the woman kind fate had delivered into his hands.

'She's not married,' Bella continued, and Julian upped her age by a year or two. Little girls didn't care about people's relationships until they were about eight. 'Are you married?'

'No, I'm not,' Julian told her, hiding a smile because he realised this was serious stuff as far as Bella was concerned. 'Maybe I could marry Daisy.'

'No, Daisy says she won't ever get married,' Bella told him. 'I know because I asked if I could be her flower-girl and she told me she wasn't getting married. Ever.'

'Maybe she'll change her mind,' Julian said, still serious although the hot pink colour in Daisy's cheeks and the way she was avoiding looking at him made him want to smile. Maybe she was coming around to the 'marriage of convenience' idea.

'Oh, I don't think so. She says she'd rather have a baby than a husband, and that's what you'd be, isn't it? A husband. My dad is my mum's husband, although he's just my dad to me. He says he can't be my husband because he's already Mum's—that's how I know.'

'You certainly know a lot of interesting things,' Julian told her, and this time he did smile.

She smiled back, but he could see the conversation had tired her so he wasn't surprised when Daisy suggested they tidy away the animals and she would read a story instead.

'If I go to sleep, will you come back later?' Bella asked her, and Daisy promised she would try.

'Though I'm helping Julian mind his sister's twins later this afternoon, so I may not make it. I think Jason and Alana are coming anyway, so you won't need me.'

Satisfied, Bella closed her eyes and listened to the story.

Daisy and Julian left the sleeping child a little later and walked quietly out of the ward.

'Will she be one of the lucky ones?' he asked.

Daisy shook her head.

'I don't know. Perhaps. If guts alone can get you through then, yes, she will be. But as you know, there's no one hundred per cent effective way of being sure there are no malignant cells lurking in the harvested bone marrow, so there's always the chance you get the child into remission, harvest cells, put him or her through hell in pre-transplant treatment, then re-infect her—in this case, with her own bone marrow.'

'Now, come on. You make it sound like a no-win situation when there *are* wins, and it does work, if only occasionally. Bella's confident, and so should you be. Don't let her down by even thinking negative thoughts.'

She turned and smiled at him.

'You're so darned nice there must be some hidden horror lurking in your depths. You're a secret drinker, gambler, drug addict—no, it can't be that, you even look healthy. Maybe a...'

'A what?' he prompted. She shrugged. 'I can't really think of any truly horrible habits or fetishes you might have—oh, fetishes. I hadn't considered that! You don't like being chained up, or beaten, or expect your partner to like it? I read a book once—'

He was laughing so much he'd stopped walking so she had to turn back.

'What?' she demanded.

'Do I really look like a man who'd like being chained or whipped?'

She studied him, then said, 'But that's just it. You don't know. I read this book where a woman assumed her husband was a perfectly normal man—not that people who indulge in fetishes are abnormal but the point was she didn't know—and then he had a heart attack in this kinky club, and she still didn't know until after he'd died and she went to the club to collect his belongings. She thought he went to a chess club every Wednesday.'

Julian was still chuckling when they reached the foyer, but thankfully he refrained from pursuing the subject in front of the other people waiting there.

Once out of the hospital, Daisy suggested they walk to the riverside park, and along it to the wharf from which the cruise would depart.

As far as she was concerned, the day just got better. Admittedly, there was an undercurrent of uneasiness sliding about inside her—no doubt, to do with making babies and compatibility and partnerships—but when she ignored it, being with Julian was as pleasant and effortlessly enjoyable as spending time with one of her close friends. In fact, the lack of tension between them—given they'd only just met and barely knew each other—was sufficiently surprising for her to remark on it.

They were leaning on the railing of the boat, having walked around the small deck in an effort to reduce the effect of an enormous lunch.

'You're very easygoing—do you ever argue? Raise your voice? Get into a fight?'

His chuckle reminded her of the full-bodied laughter

she'd heard earlier, a sound so spontaneous she smiled even thinking of it.

'Would you like me to?' he asked, and she shook her head.

'No, but it seems strange—I mean, we're virtual strangers, yet it's been so easy. At least, it's seemed that way to me. No stiff silences, no frantic searching for something else to say. No polite questions about work or travel. We've just talked.'

'And talked,' he added, smiling at her in such a way she felt warmed and cherished. Special!

Which, of course, was utterly ridiculous!

'So, what do you think?' he asked.

'About what we should do for the rest of the day?' She hazarded a guess at what he wanted to know. 'Did you give Gabi a set time you'd be back? We shouldn't be too late—she'll be exhausted. We could get off the boat when it stops in about ten minutes and get a cab back to Near West. You'd see a different view of the city.'

His smile had faded slightly, though it lingered in a teasing twist to his lips.

'Was that an innocent misunderstanding, or a deliberate red herring so you could avoid answering the real question?'

She frowned at him—more affected by teasingly twisted lips than she should be.

'The real question?'

'About our future?'

Whoosh! Air left her lungs with such force it was a wonder he didn't hear it. Teasingly twisted lips had nothing on questions like that! But she had to stand firm.

'*Our* future? Come on! I thought we'd settled that.

We might both want a child but, apart from that, we've different priorities.'

'Only because you hadn't considered the alternative,' he reminded her yet again, but smiling in such a way the alternative seemed not only possibly but positively attractive! 'How could you have, when you hadn't even met me?'

'And now I have, and have known you a little over twenty-four hours, you want an answer today?' Panic, disbelief, uncertainty—all combined to tighten her vocal cords so the words came out in a squeaky rush.

'Not necessarily, but it would be encouraging to a man who's fast becoming a knotted mess of insecurity if you could maybe give just a hint of how you're feeling about this situation. Would it help if I produced a reference? I have one, you know. My mother, fearing no one would ever have me, once wrote one out.'

Daisy blinked her surprise, especially as Julian continued speaking, as if that were a normal thing for his mother to have done.

'She wanted to assure people I was house-broken, kind, considerate to a fault, caring, could make beds, cook and even hang out washing without pulling garments out of shape or leaving big dips in the hem from peg marks.' He paused then added very seriously, 'Mum set great store by this talent!'

Daisy had to laugh, though she totally agreed with his mother. Peter had once—and only once—pegged out their washing, and his method had been to allot each article a single peg, placed randomly into the clothing so T-shirts dried with a bulge like a third breast or skirts with a bunchy bit right between the legs.

'She was right,' Daisy said gravely. 'It's certainly a

plus and something to be given serious consideration in the greater scheme of things.'

'She didn't say I didn't have any fetishes, but she was the kind of woman who'd have mentioned them if I did—if you know what I mean?'

'I'm sure.' Again Daisy agreed, though she rather doubted his mother would have known about fetishes.

'When did she write this? Was she getting desperate to have you settle down? You're what? Thirty-three? Thirty-four?'

He turned towards her and frowned with a mock ferocity that made her laugh.

'I'm thirty-one!' he growled. 'I'll have you know all Austins go grey quite early, though I haven't nearly as many grey hairs as Madeleine—just a worse hairdresser.'

'The grey's distinguished, and you barely notice it,' Daisy assured him.

And though he mouthed 'Liar' at her, she refused to be distracted.

'Well, thirty-one,' she said. 'There's a fair time lag from testosterone-laden youth, when you admit to a few minor skirmishes with the opposite sex, to now. What's happened in between? Have you been celibate or what? It's a long time—'

'Between drinks?' he offered, and she laughed again.

'I was going to say "for a man" then decided it was a terribly sexist remark.'

'It is,' he agreed, and though he wasn't smiling she sensed he was teasing her. To avoid answering her question?

'Well? What happened? There must have been other women. Why didn't they have the babies for you?'

He sighed and looked out at the greeny-brown water of the river.

'A few of them might have, had I asked, but I didn't ask because I knew they wanted more than I could offer them—knew they wanted love—and it never happened. Well, not on my side, at least. It was the see-saw effect—one up and one down. There was one woman who was different—special—and we had a relationship I thought had everything it needed for future success. I even reached the stage where I kidded myself love might exist, then one day I woke up next to Gillian and knew I didn't love her.'

He looked into Daisy's eyes and she saw something of the horror he must have felt etched in his face.

'I actually shivered, Daisy,' he said quietly, 'as the realisation swept over me. It was as if someone had poured a bucket of ice water down my back. The real horror of it was that if I'd gone ahead, with Gillian thinking I loved her—and me pretending it was true—I'd have been cheating a fine woman of the relationship she deserved.'

He paused, then added—as if Daisy needed it spelt out—'Romantic love. Hearts entwined and garlanded with flowers. That kind of love.'

The psychologist in Daisy frowned.

'Why were you so certain what you *did* feel for her wouldn't grow into that kind of love?'

He shrugged.

'I honestly don't know, but I was.' He paused, then added, 'And if you think about it, it wasn't likely to happen, was it? I'm not a believer in romantic love in the way you are. Or Gillian was, for that matter. But even if you do believe, you have to accept that it usually fades away, and you need all the things that would make an arranged marriage work—friendship, affection, compatibility, knowledge of each other—to keep a marriage going.'

'I guess you're right,' Daisy admitted. 'Though you did feel the "falling in love" urges when you were young. Did you never think that might happen again?'

Julian shook his head, shrugged, then shook his head again.

'But that was different,' he said, in the kind of patient voice people used when repeating a theory. 'It's proven that there are certain chemical changes within the body when attraction occurs, and add this to a young male's developing sexual awareness, and a certain level of emotional instability that comes with adolescence and early manhood, and you get a rush of emotion we label, for convenience, love. Unfortunately it's commercialised so much we have a culture that believes if you don't feel it there's something wrong with you.'

'You're saying what you felt for the girls who attracted you was emotional instability?' Daisy's tone echoed her disbelief.

Julian shook his head again. 'In a way. At that age, all emotions are over-emphasised. You have people looking for causes—outbreaks of nationalism, idealism, environmentalism. Young people can feel passionate over just about anything. Look at how young men rush off to war.'

Daisy heard the words and, although she could see some sense in them, to her they were more theoretical than practical. She set the unnamed young women aside and concentrated on Gillian, who had apparently been a more recent interlude in his life.

'But what if Gillian had understood you didn't love her and accepted it? If she was content to love you without being loved back? Wouldn't that have been the same as a marriage of convenience? Wouldn't that have worked?'

He looked at her as if she'd suggested walking down Main Street stark naked.

'Oh, no! It would put the one being loved under a terrible obligation. He or she would feel guilty all the time, accepting positive showers of love and not being able to reciprocate.'

Again, the psychologist considered his words and found them acceptable, but the woman in her felt a little unsettled by his certainty.

'So you're opting for a marriage of convenience. Will you write "don't ask for, or try to give me love" into the marriage contract?'

He looked puzzled by her question.

'But that's the whole point of a marriage of convenience,' he reminded her. 'It's *not* a contract of love, so there can be no misunderstandings about emotional involvement or misconceptions about romantic content in the relationship.'

'I guess,' Daisy agreed half-heartedly, wondering why this should make her feel a trifle sad. It wasn't as if her experiences of love had taught her anything other than to avoid it. Yet the feeling that someone as obviously capable of love as Julian appeared to be had lost the ability to feel it—that's what was sad.

The boat docked and she led the way to the gangplank.

'There's no sign of a taxi,' Julian remarked, as they walked up old stone steps from the small jetty.

'There's a shopping centre just up the road—we'll get one there,' she told him.

Then silence fell between them, not uneasy, just a

waiting kind of silence, as if everything that needed to be said had been said.

Though, of course, it hadn't.

She certainly hadn't agreed to his mad idea of a marriage of convenience.

Though it *would* provide her with a means towards the end she sought—and would provide her child with a caring and involved father. He and Madeleine shared genetic material and her twins were healthy, lively kids, while Julian himself was well built and obviously intelligent—very intelligent, to be admitted to an accelerated learning programme—more genetic pluses. In fact, finding someone better might be a long and tedious task, while the thought of advertising made her insides flinch.

In the cab, she named the suburbs through which they were passing.

'They're familiar to me as names but as we always lived on the other side of the river, I didn't ever know them,' Julian said, effectively killing that conversation. 'Will you come up when we get back? I'm imagining two tired and sandy little boys who'll need a bath but be fractious enough to make a solo effort difficult. I could probably cope but would rather not have to try.'

'I'll come up,' Daisy assured him. 'After all, I volunteered to help you, and having today off has already been a bonus.'

'In many ways,' he said, and reached out to take her hand, holding it lightly clasped in his on the seat between them. 'Wouldn't you agree?'

The sudden jitter in her heart was to do with the unexpected intimacy—and perhaps because she suspected he was quietly pursuing his 'compatibility' agenda. Something told her this man would be like that—laughing, smiling, talking, joking, but all the while setting a dead straight course towards whatever goal he'd set himself.

Which, at the moment, seemed to be a marriage of convenience.

With her!

Daisy laughed quietly and he turned and raised his eyebrows, inviting her to share.

And because she found it so easy to talk to him—to share—she answered.

'It's the word "convenience". We're talking about a marriage of convenience, but in the true sense of the word, wasn't it unbelievably convenient that the two of us should meet? I mean, right here and now, when both of us were contemplating a similar project.'

'Making babies?' he said, and squeezed her fingers.

The cab driver, who'd obviously been eavesdropping on what had been, until then, a fairly boring conversation, said, 'Not in my cab, thanks!'

'No, no!' Julian assured him, apparently unfazed by the remark. 'We're both too old to be messing around in the back of a cab.'

The driver chuckled, but Daisy didn't find it funny.

'I think I was always too old to mess around in the back of a cab,' she said gloomily, so Julian had to squeeze her fingers again, as if to cheer her up.

The cab drew up outside Near West as Madeleine's big vehicle pulled into the drive. While it paused for the garage doors to open, Daisy could see the twins, fast asleep in the back, while in the front passenger seat, Gabi also slept. Only Alex waved, and, judging by the enthusiasm of the action, he'd be glad to get rid of his charges.

'We should go down and help him get them out of

the car,' Daisy suggested, and Julian, who'd finished paying the cab driver, agreed.

'Gabi and Alex have done more than their share of the babysitting.'

It was the end of any personal conversation until after seven, when the tired and cantankerous twins had finally fallen asleep. Once again, Daisy slumped into the comfortable lounge and propped her feet on the coffee-table.

'Imagine if they were triplets!' she said. 'Or quads? How do those parents manage?'

'With a great deal of help from their friends, I imagine,' Julian told her. 'Would you like a drink? A glass of wine?'

'No, thanks,' she said. 'I'd probably pass out.'

'What about a spa?' he suggested. 'And much as I feel I need one to get the kinks out of my back and legs—they're so small, those children—I'd be happy to let you go in on your own if you'd prefer.'

Daisy could almost feel the warm water pumping against her tired body.

'No, that would be unfair. You get it organised and I'll slip downstairs and get my swimming costume. We can both go in together.'

'Clothed!' Julian said, but he smiled and didn't seem unduly disappointed.

'You call those two scraps of material a swimming costume?' he asked when she'd returned, been shown the spa, announced her approval of it, then had slipped out of the big shirt she'd been wearing over her costume.

Julian was glad he'd pulled shorts on over his, so the fact that his body thought they'd be compatible wasn't immediately obvious to his visitor. He turned away as she slid into the pulsing water, pretending to fiddle with the intercom, which connected to the twins' bedroom.

Then, once he was sure she'd be suitably immersed, he dropped his shorts and stepped in himself.

The situation had such overtones of intimacy his body continued to misbehave, so he was relieved—relieved and slightly put out, in fact—when Daisy asked, 'Has any paediatrician ever done follow-up studies of children born in water? Is there any data that you know of to prove they turn out healthier or more settled babies?'

He wanted to smile—mainly because the question showed just how far her thoughts were removed from his—but he was also intrigued.

'Were you considering a water birth yourself that you're asking?'

She shook her head.

'The concept frightens me. I keep thinking, what if the baby drowned, and all because I wanted to be more comfortable during my delivery? I know it doesn't work like that, and babies don't drown, but logic doesn't always hold sway against instinct, does it?'

'So why the question?'

'Because I've heard about it, read about it, and a lot of the literature suggests it might be easier for the baby—less traumatic. And supporters seem to feel that this leads to a more placid infant.'

Julian looked at her, seeing the way the steam in the room had made her hair settle into ringlety kind of curls. She attracted him—which was a bonus in terms of their possible future—but she intrigued him as well. Not many women he'd known talked so openly about their thoughts and feelings to men—particularly not to men they'd only recently met.

Perhaps the talk of a 'joint venture' between them had

done away with the barriers convention might normally have set in their path so they'd slipped effortlessly past the initial and often awkward stages of 'getting to know you' and were now at 'developing a relationship'.

'So, if I say yes, there's proof the children born in water are more content, will you override those instincts of yours and opt for a water birth for your own child?'

Daisy considered his question.

'Probably,' she replied, 'but I'd want to see the proof and consider the size of the study and any other contributing factors.'

He laughed.

'Trust a psychologist to want the facts and figures!' His leg had shifted so his toes brushed against hers, and the sensual jolt was so strong he had to be careful not to show his reaction—or let her hear it in his voice.

'But as far as I know, there hasn't been a study— well, nothing that would provide positive proof one way or the other. Of course, there could have been, but I've not come across it. Actually, if ever you have time, it might be interesting for you to go back over patient files which, for children Dr Clement has seen since neonates, would have birth details on them. Then you could judge for yourself. Actually, we've the twins on hand. Do you know how they were delivered?'

Daisy shook her head, then said, 'They were born before I shifted in. Gabi might know—in fact, she must be thinking about these things herself. Her baby's due in a couple of months. I'll talk to her.'

And as if satisfied by this decision, Daisy sank deeper into the water, which was a shame as it removed Julian's view of a deep and enticing cleavage. But the bonus was that her legs shifted so this time *her* foot brushed across his instep, the touch an accident but still encouraging.

CHAPTER FIVE

IT WAS after midnight when Daisy finally returned to her flat. Once inside the door, she leaned against it, flicked on the light and looked around at her familiar possessions and surroundings. Definitely *her* flat, *her* world, yet the 'other-world' sensation lingered.

For a start, she'd become so relaxed she'd actually felt all sexy and aroused when sitting in the spa with Julian, although the only physical touches between them had been accidental meeting of legs or toes as they'd shifted positions. In fact, if they'd sat there much longer, she might have launched herself at him, demanding they start work on 'making babies' right there and then.

Fortunately, he'd announced he was starving and had removed himself, and his most impressive body, from the spa to telephone Mickey's and order dinner for two. He had paused to check if she had any food dislikes or preferences, then had decided for her, a totally new experience for Daisy.

The meal, lamb fillets with a ginger-orange sauce on a sweet potato mash, had been delicious, the wine, one of Graham's fine cabernets, superb. But whether from the relaxing effects of the spa or the inhibition-loosening effects of the wine, the dinner conversation had been, to say the least, bizarre.

They had ranged over topics from toilet training—how young should parents start—to sexually transmitted diseases. Even now, Daisy felt heat in her cheeks as she remembered that part.

Julian had seemed more appreciative than shocked, though he'd roared with laughter when she'd first mentioned it, mainly because she'd stumbled into it, talking about Adrian and how, after finding he was gay, she'd taken herself off to be tested for every conceivable disease.

She hadn't added that it hadn't been an immediate decision, but one forced on her when she'd told Glen about her previous boyfriend and he'd insisted she be tested.

'Me, too,' Julian had admitted. 'I did it as soon as I decided I wanted to have a child. I thought with my mother's reference and a written declaration of my health, I'd have all bases covered.'

Daisy frowned as she remembered that bit of conversation—frowning over the mention of the reference, rather than his health certificate. His mother must have written it in fun. Maybe one day when he was spouting his theory that love was simply a name for the excessive amount of hormonal activity taking place in the bodies of adolescents—perhaps allied with the energy and idealism of youth.

But in Daisy's case, she hadn't stopped falling in love as she'd matured. In fact, she'd always fallen in love so easily—if disastrously—she'd virtually stopped dating after Glen for fear it might happen again.

So, wouldn't a relationship based on convenience be the way for her to go? And being married to Julian would be much the same as not dating, only she'd be able to have the child she dearly wanted as a bonus.

She shook her head, startled to think she was seriously considering his proposition.

But it did make sense. It had a lot going for it…and children deserved two parents…

As long as she didn't fall in love with Julian.

'Stop right there!'

She said the words aloud to make sure she heard them, but still her mind strayed.

The tremors she'd felt in the spa had been definitely physical—so they didn't count. Hadn't she told 'In Love' about lust and attraction?

She pushed away from the door, feeling those same tremors once again, a tingling kind of anticipation in the deepest depths of her body, like an awakening of a part of her that had slept for too long.

The sensible Daisy shook her head at this fanciful nonsense.

'Lust, pure and simple!' she told herself, turning off the light and heading for her bedroom, where she didn't bother turning on the computer because she'd promised to return to 'twin duty' at six the next morning, and if she didn't get to sleep right now, she'd never get through the day.

'Well, another day survived!' Julian said, as once again, at seven-thirty in the evening, they were slumped in the living room, breathing quiet air and listening to silence.

'Hypothetical question,' Daisy said. 'If an ultrasound were to show I was having twins, would you back away from the fatherhood deal? Perhaps jump off a cliff?' She'd no sooner said it than she raised her fingers to her lips, shocked by her own assumption that their eventual union was a foregone conclusion.

Julian smiled at her.

'I feel the same way,' he admitted. 'As if we've known each other for a hundred years and have already made the commitment to a joint future. I think it struck me when we were at the park and Shaun spread ice cream all down your top. You picked him up and kissed him better because he was upset he'd lost it, so of course it spread all over you as well, then you cleaned him up and didn't bother that your lovely shirt had green stains all over it.'

'You make it sound as if you've been looking for a messy woman all your life,' Daisy said crossly, pulling her shirt out in front of her so she could see the stains—and the dirt that had collected on them! 'You might have told me how bad this looked earlier. I'd have gone home and changed.'

'And left me with the monsters? I'm not that crazy!'

He shifted from the chair to the couch, settled beside her and put one arm along the back of it.

'Spa to clean up?' he said, but his fingers touched her shoulder and the shiver that ricocheted through her body told her it suspected he intended more than simply getting clean.

Yet she nodded, and didn't suggest going home to change.

His fingers caressed her shoulder and neck, feather-light touches that alerted all her nerve endings for further action.

'Now?' he said, and because a chaotic blend of nervousness and desire had strangled her vocal cords, she nodded again, while warning voices in her head reminded her of just what she was agreeing to.

But she *did* want a baby...

His genes would be good...

She had to start somewhere...

'Naked?'

She turned and frowned at Julian, mainly because he was interrupting her internal argument and confusing her so much she no longer had any idea what she thought or felt.

'Persistent, aren't you? Do you have to keep asking questions? Bring it all out in the open like something that needs examining? Can't we just do it?'

'Do it as in sex?' he demanded, sounding almost shocked.

'Not necessarily,' Daisy muttered, 'but you must admit it could happen. I meant getting naked and having a spa—after all, if we decide to have a baby together, we have to see each other's bodies some time, but let's just do it and not talk about it. Not plan out every move.'

'I only wanted to be sure you were ready,' he said, removing the tantalising fingers from her shoulder and tucking both hands between his knees. 'And after all we talked about last night, I thought we could discuss anything.'

Daisy pressed her hands to her cheeks as heat flooded her body.

'Yes, well, that was last night. Right now, let's just have a spa.'

Julian stood up, totally confused by where things were. He definitely wanted this woman—right now, physically—and he was reasonably certain she'd make a great mother for his children—so why did he feel he was on an out-of-control roller-coaster, hurtling into the unknown? What had happened to the rational, sensible part of his brain that ran his life so tidily?

Surely a couple of days with the twin demons couldn't have short-circuited it!

He ran water into the spa, then started the jets, but when Daisy came in and began stripping, pulling off her shirt first to reveal lush full breasts enticing even in a sensible cotton bra, he excused himself—'Forgot the intercom'—and hurried out, hoping she'd take the hint and be in the water by the time he returned.

Though then he'd have to strip off in front of her...

Had he put on weight? Were his muscles losing definition? In London he'd tried to get to the gym at least once a week, simply to keep up a minimum level of fitness, but the last few weeks...

He checked the twins—sleeping soundly—found the remote listening device and returned to the spa room. Daisy had her head back on the rim of the tub, and her eyes closed.

Didn't she *want* to see him naked?

Shaking his head at his own uncertainty, he stripped off and slid into the water.

'Great, isn't it?' Daisy murmured, her eyes still closed, her body limp with relaxation. 'I suppose if we had twins we could get a nanny.'

This practical remark, offered in a soft, sleepy, unconcerned kind of voice, had the strangest effect on Julian, an effect usually associated with far more erotic murmurings, so when Daisy's toes brushed against his legs, his own toes wanted a piece of the action, finding her leg and using touch to explore it.

'Mmm, that's nice.'

It was all the encouragement he needed. So what if the roller-coaster was out of control? He could at least enjoy this bit of the ride.

He moved closer, and now his hands explored, though he had to bite back the urge to ask her if it was OK and whether she liked his touch here or here.

'Can't we just do it?' she'd said earlier, and now he rather thought they might—before long anyway. Especially if she kept kissing him the way she was, and if her breasts kept brushing against his chest, so the sensation, intensified by the warmth of the water, was nearly driving him insane.

'I've a nice comfortable queen-size bed out there if you'd prefer it,' he whispered, when he realised their 'getting to know each other' was about to reach a whole new plane.

'No, let's try it here,' she whispered back, further fuelling his desire with a mischievous smile and a nip of sharp teeth against his lower lip. 'I wonder if a child conceived in water is more content and placid.'

The last remaining rational cell in Julian's brain was glad she'd dropped the possibility of having twins and was back to talking about child, singular, then he kissed her deeply, using his hands to both excite and move her, adjusting their weightless bodies until they fitted together in the way human beings had been so carefully and excitingly designed for.

'Oh!' she said a little later, her face flushed but a funny little smile on her face suggesting the pleasure had surprised her. Then her legs wrapped around his waist, so they were more tightly meshed together and Julian found himself voicing his own pleasure, though his was more of a groaning 'Ahh'.

They were still slumped together, replete yet not anxious to relinquish the closeness, when the phone rang.

'Hell, that'll wake the twins. I should have brought the remote in with me.'

Julian pulled away far too abruptly and was about to step out when the noise stopped and Daisy handed him a receiver.

'I noticed it last night,' she whispered as he said hello.

Daisy moved quietly away from his body, not because she wanted to break the contact but so she could take a good look at the man who'd propelled her life so abruptly in a totally different direction.

And given her body some totally unexpected but enticingly delicious pleasure!

Don't think about that. Think about the direction, which wasn't really all that different to the one she'd planned—except that the father of the baby would play a permanent role in its life, which, from the child's perspective, was good. And it had happened far sooner than she'd expected.

Her rambling thoughts were halted abruptly as Julian's side of the conversation suddenly intruded.

'Of course I'm managing. What do you think? I'd drown them both in the spa?'

He finished with more assurances, and a promise to see whoever it was in the morning, then hung up, reaching out to reclaim Daisy and draw her close again at the same time.

He kissed her wet shoulder, which caused an extremely agreeable tingly sensation in her toes, but he was frowning and Daisy could feel the tension in his body.

'What's wrong?'

He sighed deeply.

'My mother's coming!' he said in such a direful tone that Daisy laughed. 'I know. I knew that, but the reality of it hadn't struck me.'

'Why's it so bad?' she asked, though the mere thought of *her* mother visiting any time in the near future made her stomach cramp.

'She's overpowering. She's so *there*, if you know what I mean.' Julian nibbled at a bit of skin right near the base of Daisy's neck, causing new tremors to start in her pleasure centres. 'We get on well but, oh, she's so tiring, Daisy. You're such a placid, calming kind of person you probably can't imagine someone like my mother. It's like being in a cyclone that has no eye, no tiny interval of calm.'

He'd continued nibbling as he'd made this complaint, muffling the words against her skin and causing such jittery delight she had to move away, but only so she could lie on top of him and silence him with a kiss. Which led to fairly surprising developments, given what had happened only a little earlier.

But the doubt in his voice when he'd spoken of his mother lingered in Daisy's mind, while the realisation that with his parents around there'd be no more togetherness in the spa caused a contrary pang of regret in her heart.

'I don't know about you, but all this exercise, fun though it's been, has left me ravenous. I'll organise food.'

He'd obviously stopped worrying about his mother, but as he stepped up out of the spa, she could see the long, strong line of his back, and the pang deepened into something like a pain.

'And the water's making me as wrinkled as a prune,' Daisy told him, ignoring pangs and pains and pretending to be as practical about things as he was being.

Daisy took the towel he handed her, pleased he'd managed to wrap one around his waist because, no matter how intimate they'd been, getting used to nakedness was a bit daunting.

He left the room, returning with a towelling bathrobe.

'If you give me your keys, I could slip down and get you some clean clothes,' he offered, and she smiled at him.

'So I'm not caught in the lift in a bathrobe?' she teased, though once again she marvelled at his sensitivity. 'That *would* start the neighbours talking. It doesn't take much in a building as small as this. And with some of those same neighbours helping your mother with the twins…'

'Oh,' he said, and she smiled again at the stunned look on his face.

'Think about it,' she warned. 'You keep telling me you wouldn't rush me, now I'm telling you the same thing. It's unlikely I'd be pregnant already, and if I am, we can handle it. But if we were to start seriously on the making-babies project, and I do get pregnant, and if you want to be an involved father, it means a lifetime commitment to the child, if not to me.'

'But of course it's to you as well,' he said, wrapping the bathrobe around her and hugging her to his still half-naked body. 'That's the whole idea. I'd be happy to get married now, not wait until you're pregnant.'

Daisy shook her head.

'No, even if I agree to this marriage idea of yours, you want a child or children too badly for me to tie you up that way,' she said, pushing away from him because saying the words had forced her heartbeats into a panicky rapidity and she didn't want him feeling them tap-dancing against his chest.

She glanced his way, surprising a puzzled look on his easygoing countenance, then he shook his head and his ready smile reappeared, chasing away whatever thought had dimmed it for a moment.

'I'll pull on some clothes then get us something to eat. Would toast and eggs do you, or do you want something more substantial?'

Daisy picked up her watch and shook her head.

'At ten-thirty? No, eggs and toast will be fine. But let me get them.'

'Certainly not,' Julian declared. 'I'm an enlightened guy, and all for equal opportunity. Besides, if I bribe you with food, maybe you'll look more kindly on my proposal.'

If she wasn't in a parallel universe—and she was fairly certain she wasn't—then she was somewhere in a fairground, possibly on bumper cars, so her life was being continually jolted around, this way and that, directions changing so swiftly she was reeling with confusion, although the overall sensation wasn't at all unpleasant.

'Enough!' she told herself. 'Forget the fantasy and think sensibly.'

She knotted the robe and walked out to join Julian in the kitchen, but 'sensibly' just wasn't possible as she watched him industriously whisking eggs, and realised this could be the new pattern of her life. The thought brought a shiver that was more excitement than apprehension—which was just as well considering how far things had progressed between them in such a short time.

'You were saying you'd worked with Dr Clement once before. Did you get sick of face-to-face work that you left, or was the offer of a radio show too good to resist?'

Daisy smiled. She was thinking sex and marriage, and he was thinking work. Men and women sure were wired differently. But her smile faded as she considered how to respond to his question. After her experience with Glen, she'd known she wasn't up to helping others through their pain—any heartbreak story immediately reducing her to tears. So the talk-back show and the web-site had been her way of continuing to do what she loved, without anyone realising how emotionally fragile she herself had been.

'It was a combination of things,' she said, neatly avoiding a definitive answer.

'But you're ready to go back to it now?'

She shook her head, but smiled at the same time.

'You really are persistent, aren't you?'

'You'd better believe it!' Julian turned and she saw the challenge in his eyes. 'So?'

He poured the foaming eggs into a pan and continued to whisk.

'It's only a six-month job,' she said, 'and I hadn't planned to do it, but Chelsea has been very sick during the early stages of her pregnancy and decided she'd have to stop work for the duration. It was because I had worked there and knew the office and the way it works that she asked me to take over.'

He grinned at her.

'None of which really answers my question,' he said, 'but I'll let it go for now. Let's think instead about my mother. Like your fellow tenants in the building, my mother can suss out a relationship as easily as a mouse can find cheese. Will you be OK with that?'

Daisy could feel her frown forming.

'I don't know,' she said crossly. 'I mean, we don't really have a relationship, do we?'

He raised his eyebrows and she felt heat flood her body.

'Well, you might be happy to think we have,' Daisy continued determinedly, 'but I'm still not certain. Besides, you've only just arrived back in Australia. How could we possibly be having a relationship?'

'Instant attraction? Love at first sight? A lot of people believe all that twaddle.'

He was looking at her with such a teasing smile she

had to respond—to laugh—though she'd have preferred to argue over his dismissal of love as 'twaddle'.

'What about your web-site and the internet?' Julian was obviously unperturbed by her laughter. 'Unknown to the various busybodies in my family, and even, if you'd like to adopt the idea, to your friends, you and I have been corresponding for some time. We met and fell in love over the internet. Everyone's doing it these days.'

Once again Daisy felt the peculiar acceleration of heartbeats she'd experienced earlier.

Hunger, she told herself, then pointed out the flaws in his fairy-tale.

'But doesn't your mother know you don't believe in love? Do we have to have the love scenario? Wouldn't she accept the marriage of convenience—two sensible people attracted to each other, deciding to have a child or children together?'

He stopped whisking to stare at her in horror.

'Not my mother!' he said firmly. 'She's the world's greatest advocate of Love, with a capital L. As far as she's concerned, it not only makes the world go round, but I think she'd view a child conceived any other way but through love as an impossibility.'

He turned away, mainly because the eggs were catching on the bottom of the pan, then he put bread into the toaster and generally busied himself as if everything that needed to be said had been said.

But it hadn't—not as far as Daisy was concerned.

'I don't think we should pretend to something we don't feel and make up stories to give it credibility,' she said. 'But if we go ahead with this business, if we start seeing each other socially, she'd know about it, being on the spot, so to speak. So if I got pregnant and we decided to get married, it wouldn't come as a total shock to your mother. That way, she'll assume we met, got to know each other and fell in love without us actually telling her we are, or telling her we're not.'

'There are a lot of "ifs" in that sentence,' Julian said, and the serious look on his face as he served the eggs then handed her a plate made her wonder if he was having second thoughts about the project. 'Important "ifs", Daisy. "Ifs" that should be resolved before we continue a physical relationship.'

She looked at the eggs while her stomach tightened, then looked up into the deep-ocean-coloured eyes.

'Can I have a week to think about it?' she said, while her heart hammered a protest and her head told her she was mad to even consider it, reminding her of all the reasons that had led to her single-parenthood decision.

'A week,' he agreed, and for the first time since she'd met him, she couldn't see even a hint of a smile.

CHAPTER SIX

IT DIDN'T take long for Daisy to realise how much she'd missed direct personal contact with her patients. Being back in a clinic, part of a team working together to help children reach their true potential, no matter what problems they had, was far more satisfying than talking to faceless people on the phone or by email.

'Two days to go!'

Julian poked his head into the observation room where she was watching a young boy, Christian Kerr, begin an activity the occupational therapist working with him had suggested.

Daisy glanced towards the door and felt a now familiar lurch in her stomach as Julian smiled at her then walked away. Christian was unsettling the table at which he and Sue, the occupational therapist, sat by jerking his knees against it.

Ignoring the stomach-lurch, and the meaning implicit in Julian's teasing words, Daisy concentrated on Christian's behaviour and made a note on the chart she held in front of her.

But she hadn't needed words to remind her just how close the deadline had come. Sometimes it seemed she'd been ticking off the minutes—let alone the days.

She'd asked for a week, and it was up on Sunday. Today was Friday. Two more days to D—for Decision—Day.

She sighed as she noted Christian's increasingly erratic behaviour, and made more marks on the chart.

Part of the problem was Julian's mother. She was so damn *nice*. Not that nice was bad, mind you, but Mrs Austin—'Call me Diana, my dear'—was the kind of nice that made Daisy squirm, mainly because she was totally inexperienced in dealing with delightful amiability on such a scale.

And she was confiding—telling Daisy things she was sure she shouldn't know. Not that Daisy minded the stories about Julian as an infant prodigy, a child genius and a perfect teenager. But when she got onto girls he'd dated in his teenage years—'They never stuck, my dear'—Daisy felt acutely uncomfortable.

Christian left the table and was fiddling with the blind cords and suddenly Daisy's view of him was cut off as the blind slammed down.

'You're as bad as Christian is,' Daisy chided herself, as her fidgety mind wandered back to the previous weekend and the incredible interlude in the spa. Against all common sense, a big part of her wanted to say yes to Julian's proposition, for the delicious pleasure of repeating what had happened in the spa.

'That's pure self-indulgence—you're supposed to be considering what's best for the child, not your own pleasure.'

As she muttered the words crossly to herself, Sue raised the blind so Daisy's observation of Christian could continue.

The little boy was now staring into space, obviously not listening to Sue's instructions to find six blue objects on the toy shelves. He must have heard, for he crossed to the shelves, found a blue ball and a small blue truck, then he sat down and began to play with the truck, running it backwards and forwards across the carpet making *brrrooom* noises.

Two more marks on his file—one for not paying attention when being spoken to, and one for not completing his task. Christian's behaviour was leaning towards a diagnosis of ADHD, while her own symptoms were leaning towards a diagnosis of...

Marriage?

Christian flung the little truck at the wall, reminding Daisy she was supposed to be working, not contemplating her future.

'So, how's he scoring?'

Her heart pounded again at the sound of Julian's voice, but only because she was startled by his sudden reappearance in the room. Or so she told herself!

He stood so close she could feel the warmth of his body, and her nerve-endings, ever alert to his presence since the evening in the spa, sprang to attention.

'Terribly,' she said, passing the chart to him.

'Yes,' he agreed, reading then watching Christian for a minute. 'His mother described his behaviour so accurately I was sure he was a genuine case, not an overactive and possibly under-disciplined child. He's the youngest of four, so she should know what's within the parameters of normal behaviour.'

He sighed, and Daisy knew he was sighing because with a diagnosis of ADHD came the responsibility for prescribing drugs which would increase the child's attention span, and from previous conversations she knew how much he hated putting otherwise healthy children on drugs of any kind.

'I'll see you later,' he said, touching her lightly on the shoulder.

The alerted nerves prickled at the touch and Daisy thought how easily they'd slipped into a routine—her going up to help Diana with the twins when she finished work, then usually having a drink with all three Austins when the little boys were in bed and Julian had come home.

A pleasant routine, she admitted to herself, then she turned as the door opened again.

'Actually, I won't see you tonight. Christian's the last patient but I want to go up to the hospital, then I've got that association dinner tonight. Will you be seeing my mother? Will you remind her I won't be home?'

Daisy nodded. It sounded so domestic somehow—seductively domestic.

Sue had taken Christian through to Julian's office but, although there was nothing left to observe, Daisy remained in the small room, her mind once again twisting along the now familiar will-I, won't-I path.

'I think I will,' she whispered, but while her heart skittered with excitement a black cloud of doubt still hovered in her head. Meeting, attraction, lust, love, disaster—the pattern of all her past relationships. She was already through the first three stages as far as Julian was concerned, and heading, almost inevitably, towards number four. Though she hated to admit it even to herself, the more she saw of the man, the more she admired him. Especially seeing him with the twins, adapting to the practical side of caring for children, always loving but firm, even stern at times, trying theories but discarding what didn't work without hesitation.

OK, but admiration isn't love, she reminded herself, while her heartbeats accelerated yet again—this time at the lie.

But the 'I will' came under pressure that afternoon. As she helped Diana bathe the boys, the talk turned to families.

'I'm so glad Julian decided to settle in Westside and

my family is all within driving distance again,' Diana said. 'Christmas, Easter, Mother's Day—all the holidays when the family gets together have been lacking something since he went away.'

She glanced towards Daisy.

'Is your family close? Do you see your parents often? Keep in touch? I know some of my friends rarely see their children now they're grown up, but I've always believed love flourishes best in the warm confines of a family. If children receive love, not only from their parents but from their extended family members, then they will be better able to give love when the time comes. It's like a love bank,' Diana finished, turning to Daisy with a smile of pleasure at her own cleverness.

'But if you keep drawing on it, won't you eventually empty the account?' Daisy asked, relieved she didn't have to answer the 'family' questions Diana had asked earlier.

'Of course not,' Diana assured her. 'Because it keeps getting topped up. Children might not realise it, but subconsciously they must be aware of the love between their parents and that acts like a secured deposit in the bank, always there. Then the other bits, the hugs and kisses when they see Granny, the birthday card from Uncle Julian—all these things go into the account.'

Daisy sighed. Julian had mentioned his mother had strong views on love, but this strong? The concept of 'happy families' was alien enough to her, but children growing up with 'love' bank accounts?

And the 'secured deposit'—the positiveness of parental love? That wasn't going to happen in a marriage of convenience.

Diana had paused to wipe soap from Ewan's eyes. Now she added, 'It's why I worry so much about Julian.

We sent him to boarding school when he was little. It was a terrible decision because I knew he'd miss out on a lot of family closeness—miss out on love—but he was so bright he was bored to death at home. Now I don't know if it was the lack of love in his life during those years away or just his intelligence that makes him so remote.'

'Julian remote?' Daisy echoed, thinking of the man with whom she could discuss just about anything.

'Oh, people see his smile, and label him easygoing and gregarious, but behind that smile, I must admit, Daisy, he's a mystery to me. I've always feared he might not understand love, that he didn't have his love account properly established because of being sent away. I know there've been women but nothing seems to come of any of his relationships. Though maybe now he's finished his wanderings and returned to Australia, he might find someone special. Find the love I'm sure is lacking in his life.'

Ho! Daisy thought, fishing around in the bath-water to retrieve the soap. But Diana's conversation had been revealing in so many ways. Julian had mentioned boarding school, and Daisy had felt for the young boy who'd been sent away. Now she considered it, his childhood had been as deprived of close family relationships as hers, but whereas she had reacted by seeking love, his reaction had been to negate it in the grand scheme of things.

Apart from a few teenage flings which he considered an aberration of adolescence anyway!

'I would so like him to marry and have children.' Diana had continued talking, and Daisy finally tuned back in. 'Madeleine thinks she's done her bit in producing grandchildren for me, but I'd dearly love a granddaughter.'

Did she glance towards Daisy as she said it? Busy lifting Ewan's slippery body out of the bath, Daisy wasn't sure, her mind too busy, thoughts of the young Julian heading off to boarding school taking precedence over the implications of a love bank.

Diana couldn't have expected a response for she kept talking, about Julian and grandchildren and love—mostly love.

There was a lot of sense in what Diana had said, Daisy decided, her mind switching to the bank-account analogy. Her own account had started in bankruptcy and she'd tried so hard to right the situation she'd ended up in a worse financial—meaning emotional—mess. But if the initial deposit came from love between the child's parents, then entering a marriage without love would ensure the same bankruptcy for her own child.

Wouldn't it?

She worried at the problems as she wrapped Ewan in a dry towel and followed his grandmother through to the twins' bedroom, the task of dressing him now automatic.

'Will you join us for dinner down at Mickey's?'

Diana's question pulled her out of her reverie.

'I know Julian's got something on but, with Jason to babysit, Dick and I are going down. You deserve a treat after all the help you've been to me this week.'

She beamed at Daisy who couldn't fail to feel the kindness—or love—Diana Austin seemed to radiate around her.

'I'm sorry, but it's a girls' night in tonight. A few of us are having dinner at Gabi's.'

'Oh, yes, she mentioned it,' Diana said, setting Shaun on the floor and hustling both boys towards the kitchen.

Together they fed the little ones, then, as Dick—Julian's father—had returned, Daisy excused herself and went down to her flat, where she ran a bath, stripped, then settled into the warm water, lying back with her head on the edge, gazing at the ceiling as she pictured happy family holidays with the senior Austins—Christmas, New Year, Easter—with Diana overflowing with love and assuming it was the same for both her children—while Daisy and Julian pretended.

'It would be living a lie,' she told the ceiling. 'Cheating!'

'But you've been considering it—you were going to say yes,' she replied to herself.

She sighed.

'Only because you undoubtedly, in the depths of your foolish, romantic, subconscious mind, harboured hopes he'd eventually fall in love with you,' she told the unresponsive room. 'A scenario less likely now you know why he thinks the way he does—and with even his mother suspecting he's emotionally bankrupt.'

She continued to bat the mental argument one way then the other, and wasn't sure which part of her had won. Though she did know that the yes-no pendulum, which had been swinging towards a definitive yes earlier in the day, was now pointing more towards a no.

It was a shame because she wanted—rather badly—to say yes…

But if she said yes it would be for the wrong reason—not for the child or children they might have, or for Julian, who plainly wanted a mutually satisfactory but loveless relationship—but because the more she saw of him, the more she wanted to see. Yep! It was beginning to look *very* like the old pattern of her disastrous affairs.

Meeting, attraction, lust, love and disaster…

Not again!

Not ever again!

Especially not when mutual love was doomed from the start.

Problem solved, she climbed out, dried herself and dressed. She'd tell him—about the pretence, not the love—on Sunday, but until then she'd put the problem of Julian and his proposition right out of her mind. A night in with the girls was just the place to do it.

When Daisy knocked and entered Gabi's flat, Alana was over by the dining table pouring what looked like champagne. She held up an empty glass and waved the bottle towards Daisy.

'Yes, please,' Daisy said, 'but champagne? Simple extravagance or are we celebrating something special?'

'Alana's being secretive, and she's all aglow with happiness, which means she's got news,' Kirsten told her. 'It's just a matter of winkling it out of her.'

'Winkling things out of Alana isn't always easy,' Gabi reminded Kirsten. 'So how about we wait until she's ready to tell us and you bring us up to date on the latest wedding plans? Have you cut the guest list down to less than two thousand?'

Kirsten chortled with laughter.

'It's all Josh's relatives that are the problem. Apparently you can't have one without the lot, and they've bred like rabbits, that Phillips clan.'

'You could elope,' Alana suggested. 'Like we did last weekend.'

Talk about a conversation-stopper! After a silence that seemed to last for ever, her three friends all spoke at once.

'You did *what*?' This was Gabi, friend of Alana's since childhood.

'You and Rory eloped?' Kirsten made it sound like a bizarre mating ritual.

'Good for you,' Daisy offered, because on the rare times she'd allowed herself to consider saying yes to Julian, eloping had seemed the only option as far as she was concerned.

Though given Diana's passion for family, Julian might not agree...

But marriage was no longer on the agenda, she reminded herself. She'd sorted that out in the bath.

Hadn't she?

'Hence the champagne!' Alana lifted her glass high.

They toasted Alana, then she toasted them, finally explaining.

'I'm sorry if you're disappointed—you especially, Gabi—but we wanted to be married before I moved into Rory's flat, for Jason's sake more than anything. And given that neither of us have parents, and considering Jason's mother's recent death, doing it quietly seemed the best way.'

She smiled as if the memory brought great happiness.

'We went up to my grandparents' farm and a minister who's been a friend of theirs for a long time performed the ceremony. Jason was best man and bridesmaid though my gran signed as a witness as well. Then Jase stayed with them while Rory and I went to a swank hotel, booked into the honeymoon suite and did all the silly things newlyweds do.'

'Like what?' Kirsten demanded. 'Drinking champagne out of each other's shoes?'

'Yuck!' Gabi said, putting down her champagne almost untouched.

'Not out of shoes, but we did drink champagne, and we kissed and canoodled and made love in the spa.'

Daisy smiled, remembering, and naturally Kirsten saw it.

'Ha! There's a spa in the Frosts' penthouse if I remember rightly. Just look at Daisy. Did you happen to try it out while up there helping Julian?'

The others laughed, but the memory, now she'd made her decision, brought sadness. But the more she thought about it, the more inevitable her refusal seemed.

'I think she's asleep, though her eyes are open.'

It was Gabi's comment that roused Daisy from the endless circling of useless thoughts.

'Are you OK?'

Daisy hastened to reassure her anxious friend.

'I was thinking of a patient I saw this afternoon,' she said—a blatant lie but it diverted their—and her—attention.

'A little boy who'd be more trying and tiring than two sets of triplets,' she went on, remembering Christian from earlier in the afternoon and using him as an excuse. 'He's the youngest of four and so hyperactive I wonder how his mother copes. His older siblings are all OK. People argue about environment versus heredity, but children who share the same of both can be so different.'

The conversation led into the heredity-versus-environment discussion, then the pizzas arrived and food took precedence over everything else.

When the evening ended, and farewells had been said, Alana and Daisy rode down in the lift together.

'What's up?' Alana asked as they stepped out on two, and once again Daisy realised she'd been lost in thought.

She frowned at her friend.

'Why are you on this floor? If you and Rory are married, you should have got off on three.'

Alana grinned at her.

'My animals are still in my flat. We're looking for a house on acreage, but until then, for Rory's sanity as much as anything else, we're keeping on both flats. I just want to check their water.'

Daisy looked at her and waited.

'And I was worried about you,' Alana admitted. 'You've been frowning on and off all evening.'

Daisy reached out and hugged her.

'Thanks for caring,' she said, her voice husky as the emotions that bubbled too close to the surface these days threatened to overcome her. 'I'm fine. I just have to work out a few things.'

Alana hugged her back.

'If you need advice, I know a great web-site you can visit. It's interactive—you can ask for help.'

She grinned teasingly at Daisy, but though Daisy responded with her own smile, she was conscience-stricken by the thought she'd not checked the site for days.

'I might just do that,' she said, then said a goodnight and hurried into the flat.

But once inside she didn't, as she usually did, turn on her computer. Didn't even turn on a light. Instead, she crossed the living room and opened the door leading out onto her balcony, then sank into a chair and looked up at the sky. City lights dimmed the brightness of the stars, but they were still there, and Daisy gazed at them, wondering at their sparkling presence and thinking about love.

How could she not after spending an evening with three friends, all of whom had, after false starts and failures, finally found true happiness in love? Gabi, filled with deep contentment as she awaited the birth of her first baby, Kirsten excitedly planning a wedding, and Alana, lit by an inner radiance—newly married and revelling in it.

And with a sadness that welled up inside her until her heart felt about to burst, Daisy admitted to herself that all three were radiating happiness, not solely because they loved the men they'd chosen but because they were dearly loved and cherished in return—wrapped in the warm bounds of mutual love.

A taxi pulled up in the street outside and Daisy watched a big man emerge from it, bending his head back into the cab for a final word to the driver. Then he straightened, and as the cab drove off glanced up at Daisy's flat.

She sat very still, sure he wouldn't see her, but only minutes later she heard a soft tap at her door.

Open it or not?

Her legs didn't seem to think there was an option—they were already carrying her towards it.

'I thought I saw you on the balcony,' Julian said quietly, 'and hoped you wouldn't mind if I stopped by.'

He seemed hesitant, as if uncertain why he'd done it, then the smile appeared and he added, 'Actually, I had a sudden urge to kiss you goodnight.'

Daisy found herself smiling back, though it was the last thing she should be doing.

'Just a goodnight kiss?' she teased, and he laughed.

'I guess I thought it might lead to other pleasures,' he said, raising his hand and trailing his forefinger along the line of her jaw. 'It *was* a pleasure—in the spa—wasn't it?'

'It was,' she assured him, while her mind was arguing

fast and furiously. Was pleasure so wrong? And wouldn't he make an ideal father for her baby? And might not this be the last opportunity to use him this way, given what she'd decided?

She could go away, he'd never know...

No, you couldn't, her stern conscience said. No way! That's cheating! Don't even think about it!

So she looked up into his softly questioning eyes and shook her head.

He studied her for a moment, then said, 'You're going to say no, aren't you? Although the week's not up, you've made up your mind?'

She nodded, the lump in her throat too big an obstacle for words.

His eyes darkened, perhaps with anger, but when he spoke all he said was, 'Then perhaps this is a goodbye kiss.' And he bent his head and pressed his lips to hers.

Daisy felt heat simmer in her body, and she trembled with the ferocity of her reaction. Julian's big hands steadied her, one on her shoulder, the other threading into her hair, holding her head captive as he explored and teased and tantalised her mouth. Then she was clasped tightly against him, so her body knew his need was as great as hers, both of them trembling now.

It's only sex, surely there's no harm in enjoying that! the weak voice whimpered.

But she knew there was. It was like a drug, and the more you took of it, the more you wanted.

She was wondering if drug addiction—of this type—was all that bad when he released her, keeping one hand on her shoulder to steady her. Or himself!

He looked into her face, then traced the contours of her forehead, cheek, nose and chin with a forefinger, the lightly trailing touch scorching like a brand on her skin.

The second kiss was different, less desperate, yet deeper, as if a joining of lips could also be a promise—a commitment.

Eventually, he lifted his head and looked at her for a moment before speaking.

'It's only Friday, or maybe very early Saturday morning—but, whichever it is, I'm not taking your refusal as an answer. I'll ask again on Sunday, Daisy, but not until we've talked.' His eyes burned into hers, as if by their impact alone he could make her change her mind. 'And I've heard why you find it impossible to accept me as a father for your child.'

She shook her head, but didn't tell him it wasn't as a father for her child she was rejecting him but as a husband, lover, mate. And she doubted, if she practised from now to Sunday, if she'd ever be able to explain!

CHAPTER SEVEN

BUT as it happened, Sunday brought new problems and little time to do more than tell Julian—bluntly—that it wouldn't work. The disruption had begun on Saturday morning with a phone call that had hauled Daisy out of a late but uneasy sleep.

'I hate to bother you, but would you mind coming up to the hospital with me?' Julian's voice had been serious, but had still affected her. 'That's if you'd like to come. It's a newborn baby. First child, but with obvious problems. Bill Stevens, the O and G man, just phoned. The parents are very distressed and he can't contact the psychologist he usually uses.'

Daisy had taken a deep breath.

'Of course I'll come,' she'd said, hoping her voice wasn't wavering. She might have been tired and out of sorts after a sleepless night, but these people had needed immediate help and, whether she liked it or not, it was what she was trained to do.

'I have to shower and dress. You go ahead, and I'll meet you in Maternity.'

'Another ten minutes won't matter,' he'd replied. 'I'll get the car out and wait outside. We can drive up together.'

Daisy didn't argue, though she regretted it momentarily when Julian opened the car door for her and there was a shivery moment of awareness as her shoulder brushed against his chest. But that was to do with their physical compatibility, nothing more.

With the lingering lust…

'Did Bill say what was wrong? Any suspicions?' she asked, focusing her mind on work when he joined her in the car.

'Physical characteristics he first took to be Down's syndrome, but he now thinks maybe Noonan. He's leaving it to me to actually diagnose and tell the parents.'

Knowing how terrible that job must be, she touched him lightly on the arm—just to let him know she was there for him.

Julian smiled.

'You're special, you know?'

Daisy was startled enough by the compliment to ask why he thought so.

'Because you were probably enjoying a lazy morning in bed, yet you've come along more or less for moral support for me.'

'I have not! I've come for psychological support for the parents, should they need someone to talk to.'

'Would you have come for Dr Clement?' They were now pulling into the hospital car park, Julian driving carefully in the narrow lanes.

'Dr Clement wouldn't have asked me,' she told him. 'He was OK with psychology up to a point—a point that involved tests and test results—but he felt parents had to come to terms with bad news in their own way. Didn't believe in a lot of in-depth discussion, our Dr C. Though he was a marvellous paediatrician.'

'Just no good with parents?'

'I wouldn't say that. It was more that he focused so narrowly on the child, the family dynamics took a back seat.'

They'd reached the second level where parking spots were reserved for visiting specialists.

'You'll see the baby first?' Daisy asked, and Julian nodded.

Aware he was preparing himself for the task that lay ahead, she kept quiet, simply walking with him along the corridor to the maternity section of Royal Westside.

But as they walked past the regular nursery and into the neonatal intensive care unit, her stomach cramped. If she became pregnant, there was always the possibility her baby—when she had it—could need one of those ultra-sophisticated cribs.

And how would she feel if it did?

How would she handle the crisis—especially if she was alone?

Julian was speaking to the sister on duty, chatting easily, asking questions, listening to her answers. Then he crossed to a covered crib and peered in at the tiny mite inside it. He checked with the sister that the baby didn't need the small amount of supplemental oxygen the crib would provide and opened it up to lift the little bundle gently into his large, capable hands.

And in that instant, as Daisy watched the face she now knew well soften into smiling wonderment, her world stopped turning. She wasn't in a parallel universe, she was present in the real world, in a maternity unit in the hospital where she'd worked, and in spite of all her best intentions, all the warnings of both Julian and herself, she was also, undeniably, falling in love.

The knowledge flooded through her like the release of tension found in the best and most miraculous of orgasms, then the flood was followed abruptly by the reminder that her decision of the previous evening had been the right one.

Apart from her own experiences of the love phenomenon being totally disastrous, Julian didn't want love.

Julian had made 'no love' a stipulation of their relationship, and his reasoning had been spot on. One-sided love brought too much pressure to a relationship, and he had no love to give back.

At the time she'd thought it impossible—certain that everyone had love to give. But now Daisy knew his background and suspected he'd been as love-deprived in childhood as she had been, she could accept, in spite of his denials that love existed, that he did indeed have a depleted 'love account'. And maybe what he did have in the bank he spent on his small patients!

The man in question had now settled the baby on a padded bench and had gently unwrapped the small body, examining it minutely, testing reflexes, checking orifices, getting to know every wrinkle and skin cell of his new patient.

Unease turned to sadness so deep she had to close off her emotional self and concentrate on the baby.

'See this precious child. A little girl. Bill was right. She's showing a number of the characteristics of Noonan syndrome. It's something that affects about one in three thousand children—have you struck it before?'

Daisy shook her head, and Julian pointed out the widely spaced eyes, slightly downward-slanting, droopy eyelids and a broad, almost flat-bridged nose.

'Little ears, set low and tipped back, low hairline, short neck—see the excess skin at the back of the neck. But still she's pretty, isn't she?'

He was dressing her again, hands so gentle, fingers tenderly touching the elevated sternum, widely spaced nipples, telling Daisy the signs that could lead to identifying the particular syndrome.

'We'll have to do more tests, and as soon as I have her parents' permission I'll order an ECG, as she may have heart problems, and blood tests for various deficient factors in her blood. But right now we need to see her parents.'

Julian handed the infant back to the sister and, though usually very circumspect around their colleagues, put his arm around Daisy's shoulders as they left the room.

Offering comfort, she knew, but now her head had admitted she might have a problem with her heart, the wretched thing was going berserk, skipping about as if a casual arm slung across her shoulders meant he cared.

You are *not* getting involved with him, she reminded herself.

They made their way to the private room, and Julian knocked quietly, opening the door when a male voice called, 'Come in.'

The man was sitting on the bed, his arm around his wife's shoulders, and both had reddened eyes that told of their emotional state.

Julian introduced himself and was about to continue, to confirm what Bill had, no doubt, suggested, when the man held up his hand.

'We don't want to hear,' he said firmly. 'We don't want to know. We've talked about it and, though it upsets both of us to even think about it, we've decided we won't keep her.'

Daisy's body went rigid with shock, but Julian's apparent calm suggested he'd heard this reaction before.

'Children aren't like puppies, you know,' he said quietly, moving further into the room but stopping well short of the bed so the couple didn't feel their space was threatened. 'You can't actually give them back.'

The man—he hadn't introduced himself and Daisy hadn't asked Julian the couple's names—nodded.

'We know that, but there are homes, aren't there? She

can go straight into a home, where she'll be with other children like her and be well cared for. And though for us it will be as if she's died, and that's not easy...' Tears were dribbling down the woman's cheeks and the man's voice cracked as he spoke. 'We know it's for the best because we just wouldn't know what to do with her. How to look after her or help her.'

Though her heart was aching for them, Daisy had no idea what to say—where to start explaining—but Julian had obviously been here before. He stepped forward, still staying away from the bed, and pulled tissues from a box on the bedside cabinet, passing a handful to the quietly weeping woman.

'She's just a baby, and that's how you look after her and help her,' he said quietly, stepping back and returning to a monolithic stillness. 'She may have health problems which need special care, but so do many children. She will almost certainly have some developmental delay, but that's also fairly common. She could have some intellectual disability but ninety per cent of children with Noonan syndrome are in normal schools.'

He paused, perhaps letting the name of the condition sink in, then, when neither of them spoke, he continued, 'And though forty or fifty years ago, there *were* homes where children born with disabilities could be sent, as if being different meant you had to be locked away, these places no longer exist. Children who are rejected by their parents are now placed in foster-care, with normal couples just like the two of you. You would have to bear the cost of foster-care for the child yet have none of the joy of seeing her grow and develop.'

Another pause—one Daisy needed as well. She'd stopped breathing when he'd used the word 'rejected', then started again when she realised he hadn't chosen it by accident. It was used to shock the parents—a shock to counteract the shock they'd had earlier.

'Anyway, you don't have to decide anything just yet. The hospital social worker will call in to see you, and will answer any questions you might have about possible alternatives. She'll also fill you in on the government support you can access for a child with special needs and can put you in touch with parents of other children with the same syndrome, so you can talk to them about the difficulties and delights they've experienced. Sometimes it helps once you know what lies ahead.'

He turned to Daisy.

'Daisy Rutherford is my associate and she's a psychologist, so if you feel you need to talk things through with someone outside the hospital, she'll be available for you.'

The woman looked gratefully at Daisy.

'I think we'd like to do that,' she whispered, then glanced towards her husband who was still shell-shocked by Julian's revelations that he couldn't simply decide his child had died and abandon her to her fate.

Realising he wasn't going to either support or deny her, the woman added, 'But right now we're both too upset. Could you come in the morning?'

Daisy nodded, then dug in her pocket and produced a card.

'Here's my home number as well as the work one. Phone me as early as you like, and I'll come over. I don't live far from the hospital.'

The woman squeezed Daisy's hand, then smiled at Julian.

'I'm sorry if we've shocked you,' she said, 'but we were so upset ourselves, we didn't know where to start thinking.'

Julian offered her the kind of smile that could have almost cured cancer.

'You haven't shocked me. You're the people who've been shocked. You talk of grieving and that's precisely the process you must go through. You need to grieve for the perfect child you imagined having, and once you're through that, you can think about the rest.'

Another smile, this time one good enough to elicit a nod of acceptance from the man.

'Ask Daisy tomorrow about the woman who booked a flight to Italy and ended up in Holland. It's a good story.'

He glanced at Daisy who smiled to show she knew it, then he said goodbye and steered her out of the room.

'OK?' he asked, turning her so he could look into her face when he'd shut the door behind them.

'Of course,' she said, but she wasn't. There were so many things going on her head she was astonished it hadn't burst open like an overripe melon. 'I've counselled couples like them before, though never at the stage where they're still rejecting the baby. I've usually come in at the blame stage—whose fault is it?'

Julian nodded.

'Poor things, they have to go through all of that. I hope their marriage is strong enough to survive.'

It will be if it's based on love!

The thought was so strong that for a moment Daisy wondered if she'd actually spoken aloud, but as Julian wasn't looking startled, she assumed she hadn't. He excused himself, wanting to go back to the nursery, and Daisy told him she'd walk home, but as they parted, the question the thought raised—Could a marriage survive the rough bits without love?—hovered in her head.

A 'no' answer would add weight to her decision but

she knew Julian would argue that a marriage based on mutual respect would probably have more chance of surviving the problems life cast in the way.

And to prove his contention, she only had to look at her mother—from whom Daisy had obviously inherited the 'falling in love' gene—who had always married for love, yet none of her marriages—except the last as far as Daisy knew—had survived.

She sighed, then realised she had thought about her mother's most recent marriage without the usual squelch of nausea in her stomach.

Which meant she was finally over Glen!

Her pace picked up and she strode along, positively jaunty, unanswerable questions set aside while she relished this new freedom from a hangover-like angst which had lingered far too long.

For the second morning in a row, Daisy woke to the shrill demand of the phone. She rubbed sleep from her eyes and fought for control of her foggy brain.

'Hello.'

'Ms Rutherford? It's Luke Watson. You gave me your card yesterday. At the hospital. My wife and I, we had a baby... Is it too early to talk? Did I wake you? I'm sorry.'

Daisy glanced at her watch. Seven on a Sunday morning. Didn't anyone sleep in these days?

'Yes, Mr Watson, I remember. And, no, it's not too early. Would you like me to come over to the hospital now? I could be there in fifteen minutes.'

'Yes please!'

She heard relief, but it was the hint of tears still close that propelled her out of bed and into the bathroom.

'Damn hair,' she muttered a little later when, showered but still naked, she tried to reduce the mess to some semblance of order. But as she pulled her brush through it she had memories of Julian threading his fingers into it, seemingly fascinated by the unruly mass, and she ached for all the things she'd miss once she'd told him her decisions.

Up at the hospital—not long after the fifteen minutes she'd suggested, Luke Watson introduced her to his wife, Sherry, then said, 'We were wondering what Dr Austin was talking about—about Italy, you know.'

Daisy smiled.

'It's a story a woman who had a child with Down's syndrome once told, trying to explain what it was like to have a child with special needs. The story's been repeated again and again since then, so I'm sure she wouldn't mind if I shared it with you.'

She paused, settling into the visitor's chair by the side of the bed, while Luke moved closer to his wife so they were both sitting on the end of the bed, propped against the bedhead.

'She likened having a baby to going on a trip—to Italy. Planning it all ahead, buying guidebooks, thinking about what you'd see, learning a little of the language.'

Sherry and Luke nodded as if they understood this concept.

'Then, when the time finally comes, she arrives, not in Italy but in Holland. Naturally she's very upset and disappointed and angry but she's stuck there, and has to buy new guidebooks and learn another language. Then gradually she comes to see that Holland has a beauty all of its own—tulips, windmills, a quieter pace certainly, but with a certain charm. She still feels regret that she didn't get to Italy, especially as all her friends are going there and talking about it all the time. It still hurts that she didn't get to where she really wanted to go—losing a dream is very hard to cope with—but she also realises that if she'd spent all her time wishing she was in Italy, she'd have missed the beauty of Holland and all that it has to offer.'

'You're saying she's still our baby and, though she's not what we expected, she'll still bring us pleasure,' Sherry whispered.

'And pain, and heartache and a lot of extra work,' Daisy said. 'But all kids have the capacity to do that. At least you know from the start that it won't be easy and no one you talk to will tell you otherwise. But there's help available, both for her and for you.'

She looked at them, saw Luke frowning.

'Luke? Is there something you want to ask?'

'We don't know how to tell people. I mean, all our friends and relations think we've gone to Italy, if you know what I mean. How do we tell them? What will they think?'

'They'll think she's a very lucky little girl to have two caring parents who will give her the best possible chance in life. They'll be sorry for you, and some won't want to know too much, but most people will want to help in any way they can.'

'Could we talk to someone who's had a baby with this syndrome?' Sherry asked. 'The hospital social worker offered to contact someone yesterday, but we said no.'

Soft brown eyes looked pleadingly into Daisy's.

'We weren't ready,' she whispered, and Daisy nodded.

There was a knock on the door and a nurse popped her head in.

'Shall I bring baby in?' she said brightly, and Daisy

saw the same look of horrified uncertainty on both Sherry's and Luke's faces.

'No!'

Sherry answered, then, as the nurse disappeared, Luke said uncertainly, 'Maybe while Daisy's here we could—'

'No,' Sherry said again, her voice breaking on the word. 'Not yet, Luke, not yet.'

She turned and buried her head on her husband's chest, her shoulders heaving with heart-wrenching sobs.

'Shall I go?' Daisy whispered, motioning towards the door.

Luke shook his head, then nodded, then pointed towards the door as if there was more for her to do beyond it. Or maybe he wanted her to go but wait outside.

'I'll ring you later,' he said quietly. 'If you don't mind…'

Daisy wanted to hug him, hug them both, but he'd turned his attention back to soothing his distraught wife.

As she left the room, Bill Stevens beckoned to her from the nurses' station. Someone else who'd missed a Sunday morning sleep-in.

'How are they?' he asked.

'Still terribly distressed.'

Bill nodded.

'Young couple, first baby, no history of congenital abnormalities so no reason for genetic testing—it's always a shocking outcome.'

It was Daisy's turn to nod.

'His parents have been in touch with me,' Bill continued. 'They know something's wrong but not what. Luke hasn't talked to them, just asked them not to visit. They've been talking to Sherry's parents and Luke's told them the same thing. They're all very anxious. Actually, they're in the neonatal intensive care waiting room. They came up first thing this morning.'

'Is there a request somewhere in those words, Bill?' Daisy asked.

'Of course there is,' he said gruffly. 'You'll obviously be working with the parents and Julian with the baby, so rather than introduce someone else into the equation...'

'But I can't tell them things the couple might not want them to know.'

Bill sighed.

'I guess not, but often the grandparents can be the greatest help.'

'I'll see if I can talk to Luke about it,' Daisy offered. 'It's really all I can do.'

She went back to the room, tapped softly and popped her head around the door.

Sherry was lying back on the bed, her eyes closed, her body so still it was as if the most recent storm of emotion had totally drained her last reserves of energy. When Daisy beckoned to Luke, he stood up quietly and crossed the room. He looked exhausted, his skin grey with fatigue, dark-ringed eyes and stubble adding to the haunted look on his face.

'Would you like me to talk to your parents—or both sets of parents? Would that be any help?'

His eyes sparked with a tiny glimmer of light.

'Would you?' he said, grasping her hand in the tight grip of desperation. 'We've been trying to work out how to tell them but we can't—we just can't. Here, I'll give you the numbers.'

He fumbled in his pocket for a pen or paper, but Daisy stilled his hand.

'They're here,' she told him. 'I know you told them

not to come, but how could they not when they knew you were both in trouble of some kind? They're in a special waiting room. I'll talk to them there.'

She moved away, then hesitated, turning back to ask, 'If they want to see you? See the baby?'

Luke nodded, then shook his head.

'Could you come back and ask later? Sherry's sleeping now. I don't know how to answer, don't know so much...'

Daisy left, crossing to the nurses' station again to ask where the waiting room was. She was taking a deep breath and mentally preparing herself for what lay ahead when a large figure loomed in the corridor.

Overly familiar symptoms—stomach lurching, palpitations, all-over heat—arrived right on cue.

'Hi. You OK?'

Presumably he'd asked because she was still clutching the desk.

'Fine!' she said, hoping she sounded unconcerned, not demented, which was how she felt. She hauled her fingers off the vinyl and checked to see if she'd left indentations. 'I'm just going in to talk to the grandparents.'

'Like me to come with you?'

Would she ever! But maybe one person would be better—less confrontational.

'No, I'll manage. But if I can give them your number—if they want to talk to you...'

Julian's smile made her feel as if the sun was shining right here in the depths of the hospital building.

'Of course. Anything else?'

Daisy remembered Sherry's unexpected request.

'There'll be a contact number for the Noonan Syndrome Association somewhere in your office. I'd like to get hold of it today if that's possible, so I can phone and ask if someone could come up to the hospital to talk to Luke and Sherry.'

'You have done well.' Julian beamed at her. 'At least they're thinking positively. I want to see the baby, and there's another newborn I need to visit, but I was going to the office from here so I'll wait for you and take you if you like.'

Daisy hesitated, mainly because being anywhere near Julian weakened her determination to say no, then realised she had six months of being near Julian ahead of her and now was as good a time as any to learn to cope.

On top of that, it was Sunday, and wasn't the office just the place to tell him? Somewhere bland and neutral.

'That'd be great,' she said, and almost meant it. At least telling him should reduce a lot of the pressure building up inside her.

But first things first. As he nodded and walked away, she shut off all thoughts of Julian and the decision, concentrating on the tiny baby girl, whose whole future was at stake.

She took a deep breath and walked into the small waiting room, set aside for family of babies in Intensive Care. Once there, she introduced herself, explained that Luke had asked her to speak to them, then told the anxious grandparents about the little girl, explaining all she knew about Noonan syndrome, repeating what Julian had told the parents, and what she could remember from her own studies of disability.

She answered questions, talked about help, tried to ease the pain of these people who'd also suffered a loss—of the child *they'd* dreamed about. It seemed to take for ever, but she didn't want to leave them with questions still unanswered, and they seemed to need her there, as if she represented some stability in their shaken world.

'Oh, poor Sherry, poor Luke!' It was Sherry's mother, who'd been introduced as Carol Sly, who broke the stunned silence, then she turned and, as her daughter had done earlier, pressed her head against her husband's chest and cried, hurting more for the people she loved than for herself.

'Can we see the baby?'

Mrs Watson—was she Marg or Marj? Daisy hadn't quite caught it—asked the most obvious question.

'I told Luke I'd speak to him first,' Daisy said. She explained that the couple themselves were still too distressed to take it all in, but the explanation was interrupted by a knock on the door. It opened and to Daisy's total bewilderment there stood Luke and Sherry, and in Sherry's arms the tiny baby.

'We want you all to meet Isobel,' she said quietly, her voice so hoarse the words were a husky whisper. Carol moved towards the couple but Luke held up his hand.

'She's not perfect in the way some people think, but to us she's just how she's meant to be, tulips instead of gondolas.'

The four grandparents all looked stunned—no wonder—but as far as Daisy could see through the film of tears in her own eyes, Luke and Sherry were through the worst of their despair and ready to take a step forward.

Even if it was only a baby step.

Realising the family needed privacy, she slipped away.

CHAPTER EIGHT

JULIAN saw Daisy as she walked out of the waiting room. He watched her run her fingers through her hair and read the sadness and despair in her gesture. His natural instinct was to go to her and hold her in his arms, offering physical comfort and support. But even if Daisy would allow that, the hospital was hardly the place to be touching her.

Definitely not.

Especially when he knew touching Daisy was downright dangerous.

He shook his head, remembering how he'd felt on Friday evening when he'd tapped on her door after midnight, wanting her so badly his entire body had seemed to ache.

And for a moment there, as they'd kissed, he'd thought he'd won, but Daisy had refused to have any of it. And today she was going to tell him marriage between them wouldn't work.

He sighed then found a smile to greet her as she joined him near the nurses' station.

'OK?'

She looked up at him with the clear, wide-eyed gaze he sometimes saw in his dreams.

'I guess so,' she said, then she returned his smile. 'No, more than I guess so. The Watsons are, even as we speak, introducing Isobel to her grandparents.'

But the tears that leaked out of her eyes and slid slowly down her cheeks negated the smile and once again he had to clench muscles that wanted to reach out and take her in his arms.

'That's wonderful,' he said instead, inwardly cursing the ineptitude of words but finding a clean handkerchief and passing it to her. 'Are you ready now? Shall we go?'

So formal, so polite—and when he considered what they'd shared only a week ago...

Daisy nodded her agreement and walked ahead of him towards the lift, but he caught up with a couple of swift strides, falling into step with her, glancing down to see if he could see any sign that she even remembered the occasion.

'Now all we have to do is put them in touch with someone from the Noonan's Association,' she said, and he realised that even if she did remember, she certainly wasn't thinking about it right now!

She cocked her head to look up at him.

'And why are you heading for the office on a Sunday?'

So I could avoid a confrontation with you? He didn't say it but it *had* been in the back of his mind.

'I've still a lot to learn. Having Carl Clement there last week was good, but this week I'm on my own so I thought I'd go through the appointment book and check the files of the patients I'll be seeing Monday and Tuesday at least.'

They reached the car park and he held the door for her so she had to pass beneath his arm. As she did so, she glanced up at him.

'You do realise you'll give specialists a bad name, working weekends. Aren't you supposed to be greedy people who think no further than the money you can earn?'

Julian chuckled, knowing there'd been considerable media debate on just this subject. With the supposed earnings of specialists so inflated, he thought even the general public must be sceptical.

'You're doing a bit of off-duty stuff yourself,' he reminded her.

And her smile faded as she said, 'Ah, but I've a reason.'

'Like refusing a proposal on neutral ground?'

She appeared so startled that he'd guessed, he added, 'You're not that hard to read, Daisy Rutherford.'

He opened the car door for her, but once again she hesitated—almost in his arms.

'It was a proposition, not a proposal,' she said firmly, then almost to herself, as she slipped into the seat, he thought he heard her mutter, 'Unfortunately.'

But what was the difference? he wondered as he backed out of the parking spot and began the winding descent to the street. Proposals were about marriage, weren't they? And marriage was certainly what he'd proposed.

'Well?' he demanded when he realised his mind was only arguing semantics because of the anxiety tightening his gut.

She glanced his way as if she didn't understand.

'The car is neutral ground—you can tell me here.'

Her hand lifted as if she was about to touch him, fluttered for an instant like an uncertain bird, then dropped back into her lap.

'OK!' she finally responded. 'I can't marry you.'

'Can't or won't?' Semantics again.

'Won't—can't. It amounts to the same thing, surely.'

A quiver in her voice suggested saying this was no easier than hearing it.

He waited, wanting to demand to know why but guessing silence would work better than a demand. Silence was a trick she used herself—to good effect.

'There are so many reasons I don't know where to begin,' she said at last, sighing as the words faded into the air between them. 'I suppose, with honesty.'

She turned to face him, and as he pulled up at a traffic light he looked into the usually crystal-clear eyes, and saw the clouds of doubt and worry.

Sorry that he'd caused them, he touched her cheek and drew his finger along the line of her chin.

'Honesty?'

She shifted so his hand fell away, and waited until the lights changed and he had to concentrate on driving, before she added, 'Honesty in life—in deed, I suppose I mean, rather than in word. You said much the same when you talked about Gillian—that you'd be cheating her if you let her believe you loved her. I listen to your mother talk about love, I look at my friends, I imagine us at social or family events and know that while the happiness I see all around me is genuine, ours would be fake.'

'Hey!' Thank heavens he'd reached the office. He pulled up in the deserted car park and switched off the engine before turning towards Daisy.

'You're thinking emotionally rather than rationally. There's nothing to say our happiness wouldn't be as real as anyone's,' he protested. 'The whole idea was to make us both happy—to have the baby we both want, and give the baby two parents instead of one. Do you think living with me would make you unhappy, Daisy? So unhappy you'd have to pretend?'

Daisy looked at him, seeing concern in his face and a hint of anger in his eyes.

She knew living with Julian had the potential to make her particularly happy—but it had even more potential for disaster, though she wasn't going to admit that right now.

'Happiness was the wrong word,' she said, tension tightening her skin until it prickled. 'It just seemed like a better way to explain.'

'And what was the right word, Daisy?' he asked, his voice like silk, sliding across her prickly skin.

'Love!' she muttered, then, angry that he'd forced the issue, she looked up and glared into the eyes she usually found so mesmerising. 'There, I've said it. If we married, all the people I care about, all my friends, and now your family, too, would assume we married for love, and that's a pretence I don't think I could handle. OK? Especially not with a man who refuses to admit love even exists and puts whatever relationships he has had down to hormonal glitches! You're an intelligent, programmed machine, Julian Austin. A robot, not a man.'

She snapped open the door and got out, marching across the car park towards the front entrance of the low-set building. Which was when she realised Julian's key was probably for the staff entrance around the back.

She turned to see where he was heading.

Nowhere!

He was sitting in the car, his elbow resting on the window-sill, his head propped on his hand. She studied him, trying to analyse the pose. Did it show relief?

Acceptance?

She hoped the latter as she certainly didn't want to tell him her other, far more compelling reason for refusing him. The one about the pattern of her relationships—the meeting, attraction, lust, love, disaster scenario.

She suspected she'd probably gone past the point of

no return and disaster loomed ahead, but one thing experience had taught her was that eventually she'd get over the disaster and learn to live again.

Even with Glen, she reminded herself, as a very different man climbed slowly out of his car, shut the door and locked it, then turned and waved her towards the back entrance.

'I imagine the address you need is in the files in the main office,' he said, as if she hadn't just refused to marry him.

Or as if it didn't concern him one jot that she had!

And why should it?

He was attractive, well off and a thoroughly nice man—there must be thousands, if not millions of women who'd marry him without a second thought.

And on his terms!

'Thanks,' she said, but some of the dismay her thoughts were causing must have found expression in her voice for he glanced her way—a quick but searching look—then touched her lightly on the shoulder.

'Don't fret about it,' he said quietly.

Julian unlocked the door and held it open for her while trying to analyse what he was feeling.

Anger—how dared she call him a machine?

But disappointment as well. He wanted a baby, she wanted a baby, they had work in common. It had seemed so perfect. Yet the disappointment was tempered with something else.

Disbelief?

Why disbelief?

His analytical mind did a quick scan of the parts of his brain he rarely considered, the parts that governed things you couldn't quantify—like emotions. But the scan came up with no rational reason why he should be feeling disbelief.

He reminded himself he'd known since Friday that Daisy intended saying no, but that didn't help. Anger faded to an irritable tetchiness as he reviewed the week that was.

Damn the woman!

He walked through to his office, the appointment book and files forgotten, and slumped into the chair behind his desk. But after only a week working with her, the ghost of Daisy was firmly installed in his office and he could see her in the chair across from him—as she had been last Tuesday when they'd discussed suspected child abuse.

He remembered her emotion-charged voice as she'd declared everyone was responsible for protecting children, and, remembering, he understood what she'd meant about pretence. Though their acquaintance was only ten days old, he already knew that Daisy threw herself whole-heartedly into everything she did. The story of her past relationships was enough to prove that. What you saw with Daisy was what you got. Pretence was an alien concept.

And she couldn't pretend she was in love with him? Was that what she'd more or less said?

The thought made him feel cold, old and distinctly uncomfortable—so much so he twitched his shoulders in an attempt to make his skin fit better.

It also caused a strange ache in his stomach, but maybe that was an ulcer developing.

He considered the possibility then dismissed it as irlevant, his mind—which always asked why—turning instead to why she couldn't pretend she was in love with him.

Well, he knew why she couldn't pretend, it wasn't part of her make-up, but what if it wasn't pretence? Why was she, the great love advocate, so certain she wouldn't ever fall in love with him?

He was reasonably certain, if he were a believer, that Daisy would be just the kind of person with whom he'd fall in love.

But on her side, was he so unlovable?

Or was she still in love with number three—the man she didn't talk about? She'd said he wouldn't be returning, but not why.

Too many questions.

Julian pushed himself to his feet and walked out to the reception area where Daisy was still on the phone, though the thanks she was offering suggested the conversation was nearly finished.

He waited, pretending to look at the appointment book, and when she'd finished said, 'I don't suppose you'd have lunch with me.'

She looked at him, her eyes wide and startled, her face a pale moon in the dark cloud of her hair.

'Why?'

He smiled at the question.

'Does there have to be a reason?'

'Usually.'

The clear eyes were hooded against him, a fringe of dark lashes hiding whatever she might be thinking.

'I'd like to talk.'

She looked up then, the fringe lifting, her eyes, pale green today, studying him as if she might read his thoughts in his face.

But whatever she saw there couldn't have satisfied her, for she shook her head.

'I don't think talking's a good idea,' she said quietly,

and he sensed strain in the tightness of the words. 'Anyway, I'm going back to the hospital. I want to introduce the woman from the Noonan Association to the Watsons. I'll walk back—I need the exercise.'

Thus dismissed, there was nothing left to do but pick up the appointment book, then find the files he needed.

But hard though he tried to concentrate, an image of Daisy's face, wide-eyed and pale-skinned, continued to float, like a disembodied ghost, between his eyes and the written words.

It became the pattern of his days. Though the real Daisy was there as often as the ghost.

Annoyingly, she gave absolutely no indication of how she was feeling, carrying on as if the brief, and to him quite special intimacy between them had never happened. Yet the more he saw of the real Daisy, the more convinced he became that she was perfect for him. This led to intense aggravation—that he, a man who supposedly had a genius-level IQ, had made such a hash of things he'd lost her.

There was a tap on the door and the 'her' in question poked her head in.

'Do you want me for the parent information evening you're running tonight?'

Hearing the first four words, it was hard to bite back a growl. Aggravation was one thing, but when it was exacerbated by frustration it was no wonder he was getting an ulcer.

'Parent information evening?' he repeated, trying to make sense of the words while his body went through its 'responding to Daisy' routine.

'For the Children With Special Needs Support Group,' she said, brushing hair back from her face in a move calculated to remind him just how soft that black mass had felt against his fingers and tighten the stirring in his body to active need. 'You said they could meet here.'

'That's tonight?'

He *was* growling now.

'At eight,' she said, calmly enough, though her eyes narrowed and she glanced around as if to see what had upset him.

As if she didn't know!

She couldn't be as unaware as she pretended, this woman who hated pretence!

He frowned at her, then realised she was waiting for an answer.

Genius IQ and he couldn't remember the question.

'Did you want me tonight?'

He remembered as soon as she spoke, but this time the phrasing licked fire through his guts.

'Yes!' he said, and meant it.

Though she looked startled by the roughness in his voice, she apparently took his reply at face value—thinking of the meeting—for she nodded calmly and said, 'OK. The secretarial staff won't be here so I'll come in earlier and put on the urn, see to chairs and such. Although it's a non-specific group, I think Luke Watson wants to come. I was talking to him earlier today. Sherry's been discharged but she's visiting the hospital each day, expressing breast milk for Isobel.'

She backed away, leaving him staring at the place where she'd been, but this time the ghost was absent and all he saw was an empty doorway.

Daisy sighed as she retreated. She was surviving working with Julian by keeping out of his way as much as possible. But many of her subterfuges failed. Like when she emailed him a question, then found him coming to her office in person to answer it, or when she ducked away from the penthouse, where she still helped Diana with the twins, before he came home from work, only to have him knocking on her door a little later with something she'd left behind or a message from his mother.

Had it been anyone but Julian, she'd have suspected he was seeking her out, but he'd accepted her refusal without argument, and seemed totally unaffected by it. So it must be her imagination—and her own anxiety to hide her true feelings—making her feel he was haunting her.

She headed home, pleased, for once, to have no 'twin duty'. Gabi was taking the twins to a performance of the Triple Ts, stars of a children's television show the two boys loved. So she was free to have a long bath, wash her hair, do some general body maintenance stuff before…

She sighed again.

Before once again putting on her happy face for the benefit of Julian Austin?

With a pang of guilt she remembered the parents who would be at the meeting, and the difficulties they faced. She could be of real help to these people, so she had to forget Julian and act like the professional she was.

Thus fortified, she climbed the stairs to her floor rather than taking the lift, then, as she put her key in the lock, she heard the phone.

Naturally, she fumbled, but it was still ringing as she grabbed the receiver.

'Daisy? It's me, Glen.'

Heart, lungs, brain all stopped working, though something—automatic response maybe—managed to produce a garbled, 'Glen?'

Thank heavens she hadn't said, 'Glen who?'

'It's your mother. She's had a heart attack. A bad one. She's been transferred from the coast and admitted to Royal Westside. I thought you should know.'

Daisy slumped onto the couch, her legs no longer able to support her, and held the receiver to her ear as if it might somehow explain to her why she was feeling so stricken. But though she thought she could hear Glen breathing on the other end, he didn't speak, and in the end she knew she had to do something—say something.

'I'll be there in ten minutes,' she said, and heard what sounded like a sigh of relief.

Still dazed, she dropped the phone back into its cradle, then stood up, checked her handbag was still slung over her shoulder and her flat keys still in her hand, and walked towards the door.

Familiarity took her feet towards the hospital, a walk she couldn't recall when she looked back later. Glen was in the CCU waiting room. He looked up, but the hope in his eyes died when he saw it was her.

'I didn't know if you'd come,' he said, shaking his head.

Daisy crossed the room to sit beside him.

'Of course I'd come,' she said, wanting to touch him, to offer physical comfort, but not knowing how to do it, given the strain between them. 'Have they told you anything?'

'Only to wait,' he said harshly. 'What are they doing in there? Why won't they let me see her?'

Daisy heard the agony in his voice and realised he still loved her mother—and how much it was hurting him to know he couldn't take away her pain.

'They'll come as soon as they have something to tell us,' she said gently, trying to remember what she knew about heart attacks. During her studies, she'd read specific information, as it was common for patients to suffer psychological problems, such as anxiety, following such massive disruption to the functioning of their bodies. And before a psychologist could treat such patients, he or she had to know where they were coming from and understand the event.

'I think right now their main concern will be to stabilise her. The pain of a heart attack is caused by the heart not getting enough oxygen, but the pain makes breathing harder so the heart gets even less and tries to work harder so it hurts more, and it's a vicious cycle. First the medical people give something to stop the pain, and provide supplemental oxygen so the heart doesn't have to work so hard, then they try to limit the amount of damage done to the heart muscle, because heart muscle doesn't recover.'

'Keep talking—it helps,' Glen muttered, and again Daisy had to search her mind for information. Hadn't Gabi once explained it when they'd been talking about the Golden Hour, the time paramedics sometimes had to save a patient?

'The problem is that nitroglycerin and morphine, traditionally used together to treat the pain and lower the blood pressure, dilate the blood vessels all through the body, not just those near the heart. If blood pressure drops too low, and the brain doesn't get enough oxygen, it panics and can cause another heart attack.'

Glen groaned as if the thought caused him physical anguish.

'That's why they monitor every bit of medication, and the reactions, and need to stay alert to the patient's status all the time. As long as it's fluctuating—as long as her blood pressure isn't stable—it's more important that there are specialists with her than family.'

'I wouldn't be in the way,' he argued, and this time Daisy did touch him, resting her fingers lightly on his arm.

'They'll call you as soon as they can,' she assured him.

'I suppose so,' he conceded, 'but how long can all this take?'

Daisy didn't know though she guessed the longer it took to stabilise a patient, the more chance there was of serious complications, even full cardiac arrest.

The thought made her feel physically ill, and she dropped her head into her hands and prayed it wouldn't happen.

CHAPTER NINE

IT WAS another hour before a nurse arrived, to tell Glen he could visit his wife.

'Five minutes only,' she said, as she led Glen to the room where machines monitored every function of his wife's body. 'She may not be aware of your presence, but talk to her anyway. We believe it helps.'

Daisy walked with him to the room, and looked through the glass at her vibrant, energetic mother lying so motionless on the bed she seemed like someone else. She saw Glen take her hand, and his lips move as he spoke, and Daisy's heart ached when she saw the mix of love and helplessness on his face.

At ten o'clock, the specialist pronounced Mrs Carlton out of danger, and after Glen paid a final visit to the slumbering woman, Daisy persuaded him to go back to her place to get some sleep.

'I'll stay here and phone you if there's any change. You can be back here in ten minutes if you're needed,' she assured him.

'But I should stay,' he protested, though his words were ragged with exhaustion.

'No way! You're not going to be any use to anyone tomorrow if you don't get some sleep, and if I know Mum, she'll bounce back and be demanding attention from the moment she wakes up.'

A faint smile glimmered on Glen's tired face, but he didn't argue as Daisy jotted her address down on a scrap of paper and gave him verbal directions for getting to Near West.

'Phone me if there's any change at all,' he repeated, as she walked him to the lift. 'And if I don't hear, I'll come back as soon as I wake up.'

'I know you'll want to, but grab a shower and something to eat before you come. You'll be in for another long day.'

She watched him go, and imagined him walking back to the flat she'd fled to when he and she had broken up, and all she felt was pity that he was suffering so much.

Halfway through the parent meeting, Julian's anger with Daisy—how dared she not turn up when he'd specifically said he wanted her there?—deepened to concern.

It wasn't like Daisy to let anyone down. In fact, she was the last person who'd do such a thing.

He'd phoned her number when he'd arrived to find no chairs in place, no urn turned on, but there'd been no response, and she didn't have an answering machine on which to leave a message.

Somehow he got through the talk and survived the question time—even delayed his departure to speak to Luke Watson for a few minutes. But the moment the last person was gone, he switched everything off, locked up and drove, too fast, to Near West.

Noises from Mickey's Bar suggested a party might be going on in there, but he didn't hesitate even long enough to peer through the door, instead taking the stairs two at a time to the second floor.

He hammered on her door, wondering what he'd do if Daisy didn't answer.

Which she didn't, so he knocked again. This time he thought he heard movement from within.

But when the door opened it wasn't Daisy but a man, naked except for a towel clutched around his middle.

'Daisy's not here. I'm Glen,' the stranger said. 'She's at the hospital. Her mother's had a heart attack.'

He then shut the door, leaving Julian in the foyer, standing motionless.

Glen. His memory obligingly provided him with the conversation where he'd heard the name. He was the third man in Daisy's list of disasters. The one she'd assured him would never make a come-back into her life.

Yet here he was, naked in her flat!

Obviously the first person she'd turned to when her mother had been taken ill and she'd needed someone.

And she had the hide to talk about pretence!

Hot acid churned in his stomach, making it clench with the pain. His cool, calm, analytical mind decided it must be the ulcer, but another seldom-used part of his brain refuted this, suggesting it might be an emotional reaction.

He backed away from her door, startled by such a bizarre thought.

An emotional reaction?

Like what, for instance?

Anger?

Jealousy?

He shook his head, dismissing the idea.

But he dithered in the foyer, uncertain what to do next.

Because he was concerned for Daisy, he told himself, not for any other reason.

He made his way up to the penthouse, letting himself in, then taking the phone into the kitchen so he could phone the hospital without waking anyone. But Royal Westside had no female patient called Rutherford.

He searched the phone book for private hospitals, uncertain how many of them would be large enough to have a coronary care unit.

In the end he phoned them all anyway, with no luck.

Then another memory surfaced—had it been the pancake morning? He thought so, but clearest of all was Daisy's voice—'My mother went from man to man.' If she'd married any of them she wouldn't be Mrs Rutherford. All his efforts to track her down had been wasted.

He groaned with frustration.

By now, it was close to midnight and, knowing there wasn't a darned thing he could do, Julian took himself grumpily off to bed, where sleep failed to soothe his concerns because the ghost Daisy floated through his dreams while the need to be near her—to at least offer help or comfort—ached like an illness in his bones.

By five, he decided it was better to be awake than asleep, and he got up, moving quietly so he didn't wake his parents or the twins, showering, dressing and leaving the apartment in the minimum of time.

He'd go up to the hospital and see Isobel, and the other newborn who was his patient.

And it wouldn't be far out of his to walk through the CCU at Royal Westside.

The relief Julian felt when he saw Daisy in the CCU waiting room was beyond any rational reaction, though relief was immediately followed by the now-familiar heartburn feeling when he realised the other person in the room was Glen.

And *he* was holding Daisy's hand. Offering the comfort Julian wanted to give.

He hovered just outside the door, wanting to speak

but not trusting his voice—it would probably vibrate with anger, the way he was feeling right now.

Not that the pair in the room would notice, any more than they'd noticed him standing there. Daisy's whole attention was focused on the man who'd hurt her, yet, now he looked more closely, her body language suggested she was the one offering comfort.

Then he heard the words and, though he knew it was wrong to listen to someone else's conversation, he couldn't walk away.

'I love her so much, I don't know what I'd do if she doesn't recover,' Glen was saying, his head bent forward, his shoulders bowed, his voice muffled by emotion. 'I know what we did to you was terrible, Daisy, but we didn't do it deliberately, you must know that. It just happened, and it would have been useless to deny it.'

Daisy's murmured reply was inaudible, but Julian doubted he'd have heard anything at all, given the roaring in his head as he assimilated the meaning of the words.

She'd talked about the other two losers in her life, but this? For a man she'd loved—a man she'd thought loved her in return—to betray her with her own mother...

Yet she still had faith in love?

Believed in its existence?

He looked at her, the dark head bent towards the useless lump of ectoplasm who'd hurt her so deeply, offering him comfort he definitely didn't deserve.

She was wearing the skirt she'd worn the day they'd gone on the boat, and, recognising it, he realised she must have been here all night—been here since she'd left work the previous day—for she was still in the same clothes.

Concern for her propelled him into the room.

'Daisy?' he said softly.

She looked up, startled at first, then frowning at him. 'Julian?'

She stumbled to her feet, and he reached out to steady her, grasping her hand and feeling the pressure of her fingers.

'Is something wrong? Is it Isobel?'

He had to smile. It didn't seem to matter what the situation, she always thought of others first.

'No, she's fine. Everything's all right, but when you didn't turn up last night I was worried.'

'Oh, the meeting!'

He was still holding one hand, but the free one went to her mouth, pressing against her lips in concern. Tired grey-green eyes lifted to meet his.

'I'm sorry, Julian. I should have phoned. My mother...'

He squeezed her fingers and drew her closer, pulling her into his arms and holding her against his body, feeling her weight slump against him, her head rest on his shoulder.

'I know,' he said gently. 'I called at your flat last night. Glen told me. That's why I came.'

She pushed away, her head lifting and her eyes once again meeting his, but this time with a puzzled frown.

'It's why you came?' she repeated, her voice as puzzled as her eyes.

'To see if there was anything I could do,' he said, his fingers going to her chin so he could tilt her head and study her face. 'Have you eaten? Can I bring you something? Or, better still, take you down to the canteen?'

A glimmer of interest sparked in her eyes and he pushed the advantage.

'A break away from here might do you good.'

She smiled, a weak effort but enough to tug at something in his chest so his heart felt like a balloon cut adrift from its moorings.

'You've talked me into it,' she said. 'I'll just tell Glen.'

She nodded towards the man sitting slumped in a chair against the opposite wall of the small room.

'That's Glen, my mother's husband.'

So his guess had been correct, Julian thought, managing to nod acknowledgement of Daisy's halting, 'Glen, this is a friend of mine, Julian Austin.'

The man stared blankly at Julian, perhaps trying to place him, then nodded abruptly.

'I'll be back in fifteen minutes,' Daisy told Glen. 'Can I bring you anything from the canteen?'

He didn't look at her, just shook his head and continued to slump in his chair, his hands clasped between his knees, his head bent low as if counting the tiny spots in the linoleum beneath his feet.

'He's so worried, he must really love her,' Daisy said as they walked out. She was obviously concerned on the rat's behalf.

But that was Daisy, soft-hearted and trusting.

Julian felt obliged to put his arm around her, and, holding her protectively close, he took her not to the canteen but to the coffee-shop just inside the main entrance.

'You're probably on caffeine overload after a night in a waiting room, but what about a cup of tea and perhaps a Danish pastry—loaded with carbohydrates to keep you going?'

She moved away from him and turned to smile, and he felt as if the world had shifted focus so all he could see was a tired, pale-faced, dark-haired woman, with shadowed, silvery green eyes. And looking at her, he felt his heart move again so that, in spite of all the scientific data that disproved such a thing as love existed, he had to wonder if perhaps science had got it wrong.

'Sit here, I'll get the food,' he said, steering her to a chair and all but shoving her into it, in case the tumult he was feeling was showing in his face.

Daisy sat, content to be ordered around. The sight of her mother, the liveliness that was so much part of her beauty denuded by her unconscious state, had shocked her, while the tubes and monitor leads and paraphernalia so familiar to anyone who'd worked in a hospital seemed somehow alien when attached to a person she knew and loved.

Still loved in spite of what had happened, for who could not love a creature so vital and full of love herself?

Regretting the time they'd lost, when she had held herself apart, Daisy brushed away a tear. Then Julian was back, handing her a handkerchief, touching her shoulder, her hair, telling her in so many ways he was there for her.

'I'm OK,' she told him, 'just made miserable by regrets, and that's a waste of time. We can't alter the past, but we can do better in the future.'

She paused, took a deep breath, then added softly, 'Let's pray there is a future.'

'There will be,' he assured her. 'Think positive.'

'I was until she had a second attack early this morning,' she said bleakly. 'I'd sent Glen home to sleep but had to call him back, and now we're at the waiting stage again.'

He took her hand and gently squeezed her fingers.

Daisy disentangled her hand but smiled her gratitude,

and watched a subtle change of expression on Julian's face—as if a switch had been flicked, but whether on or off she couldn't tell.

'There,' he said, 'I've cut the Danish for you. Now all you have to do is eat it.'

He pushed the plate towards her.

She ate a quarter of the pastry, because he was trying so hard to help her, then said she had to go, anxious to be closer to her mother—and equally anxious to be away from Julian. Being with him like this, being cared for so considerately, exaggerated the regret she already felt about saying no.

Not that there'd been any alternative.

He walked with her back up to the CCU waiting room, arriving just as a nurse walked in to tell Glen he could see his wife.

'She's stable, but sedated. She's been through a lot.'

Daisy waited until he left, then slumped into a chair.

'She won't even know I'm here. How stupid to have wasted the years since it all happened. He obviously loves her deeply—and I guess it wasn't either of their faults they fell in love. It had to be fate—something that's meant to be—worked out by a cosmic pattern too big for us to comprehend.'

She looked despairingly at Julian.

'But surely you can see now why we shouldn't marry—why the convenient marriage isn't such a good idea? Glen and I thought we loved each other, then he fell—really fell—in love with someone else. You and I, well, not loving me in the first place, there'd be no barrier at all if you met someone and fate decreed, in spite of all your rational denials of love, you fell for her.'

Julian heard the words and could see where she was coming from—from the pain of past betrayal. But now there was another dimension to the problem. If love did exist—and he wasn't quite ready to accept it did—then to offer Daisy love, when her experiences of it had been so shattering, might frighten her away.

The thought sent an icy trickle down his back, although the rational part of his brain was reminding him she wasn't his to frighten away.

She'd said no.

Ignoring it, and the other mental nudge that suggested he should be on his way to work, he sat down beside her.

'Listen,' he said quietly. 'If you were to change your mind—say yes instead of no—you need have no fear that I'd ever let you down.'

He turned her head and kissed her gently on the lips.

'Never in a million years, and no malign fate or cosmic pattern could make that happen—understand?'

Daisy looked at him and he saw a kind of wonder in her eyes, as if she wanted to believe what he was saying.

Then she shook her head, but whether dismissing his words or her own thoughts he couldn't tell.

'You'll be late for work,' she said, and he smiled and kissed her again.

'Practical Daisy,' he teased, but he stood up anyway. 'Phone me if you need me for anything,' he told her. 'A lift, a meal, company. Particularly company.'

She smiled, a tired, wan effort but still a smile, and Julian carried it with him out of the room, and right through a very busy day.

Daisy watched him go, her heart aching because she knew it was Julian's innate kindness, not love, which had prompted the visit.

She waited until Glen returned from his allotted time with her mother.

'She seems better, and she knew I was there,' he said bleakly, 'but the doctor says it will be a while before she's properly aware of what's happening around her. With only five minutes an hour allowed for visits—'

He stopped abruptly, slumping back into a chair, but Daisy knew what he was holding back. He wanted all those precious five minutes.

'You'll do her more good than I would,' she said, conceding this was true though it hurt to admit it. 'I think I'll go home and have a sleep. You've got my number. Ring me if there's any change and, please, Glen, give her my love. I mean that!'

He looked up at her and nodded.

'I know you do,' he said. 'And thanks.'

She walked away, pausing outside her mother's room, thinking maybe Julian was right. If you thought rationally rather than emotionally, and reduced love to mere chemical changes within the body, think of all the pain you'd avoid.

'Oh, Mum,' she whispered as she studied the still figure, all the pain she hadn't avoided swamping her tired body.

Daisy woke at three, heavy-headed and confused. Had a shower and washed her hair, but even that failed to make her feel any better.

Phoned the hospital. Her mother was improving. Visits had been extended to ten minutes an hour and Mr Carlton was in with her now.

And though she felt genuine relief, even that news failed to cheer her.

Well, it would be an hour before her mother could

have another visitor, probably three or four before Glen would give up his precious ten minutes.

Daisy made a cup of coffee and started up her computer. It seemed like days since she'd checked her emails and web-site. Maybe sorting out someone else's problems might make her feel better.

As she'd expected, the question box was full, so she settled on the bed and began to read the first request, because she tried, whenever possible, to answer each question in order, completing one before moving on to the next. Early on, she'd found that if she read the lot, she'd pick out the most interesting request and answer it first, usually giving it more time than the less challenging queries. Answering them in order, it at least gave every questioner equal thought and time.

The first was from a sixteen-year-old girl who wanted to know about the symptoms for STDs, as if all sexually transmitted diseases showed up in the same manner.

Daisy explained she wasn't a medical doctor but, having been asked so many times before, she was able to give a web-site where the girl could access more information. She ended with a reminder to see a live doctor for a proper diagnosis and what she hoped was a scary explanation of how unprotected sex could seriously muck up a young person's life.

The next question was from the mother of a six-year-old bed-wetter, and though this was also a medical problem, Daisy had dealt with it often enough to know some of the answers. She made some suggestions the woman could try, waking the child a couple of hours after he went to sleep usually the most effective, then suggested seeing a doctor to check there was no physical problem causing the bed-wetting.

Part of her was glad the backed-up questions were so

practical. She could set her mind to answering them without any emotional input at all. Then she reached the third, and realised her luck had ended. The enquirer—'Just Asking' was the pseudonym he or she was using—wanted to know how you could tell you were in love.

'I'm a psychologist, not a marriage counsellor,' Daisy muttered at the screen, but the question gave her pause. 'You want my view, or some professional approach, JA? Personally, it makes me feel sick when I see the person I love unexpectedly. It makes my heart race, and my lungs tighten, and my knees go boneless so I have to reach out for support. The esteemed and very intelligent Julian Austin, however, would tell you those are mere chemical reactions inbuilt in humans to ensure the continued survival of the species.'

She was still staring at the screen when there was a knock on the door.

'I thought you might be home,' Alana said, smiling at her. 'Are you OK? I heard about your mother—Julian told Diana who told Gabi who told me. I'm so sorry. Is she OK?'

Daisy nodded.

'She's still in the CCU but improving slowly. I was doing a bit of work before I went back up.'

'That's why I'm here,' Alana told her. 'I thought you might like some company before you return. Let's go down the road and stock up on caffeine.'

Only too pleased to have an excuse not to think—particularly about love—Daisy closed down her computer, grabbed her jacket and joined Alana, walking down the stairs because Alana was into fitness and rarely used the lift.

'How did you know you were in love?' Daisy heard herself ask as they rounded the first landing.

So much for not thinking about it! She'd managed all of sixty seconds.

Alana's smile revealed her thoughts, and Daisy hastened to make amends.

'Not for me,' she said firmly. 'Heavens, I've been in love often enough, you'd think I'd know, but I've been so wrong I can't trust my judgement, so I thought I'd get a second opinion. It's for a web client, someone calling herself—or himself, I suppose—"Just Asking".'

'Oh, your web-site! But surely you answered those questions on the radio. In fact, you did, because I've heard you at it.'

'On the radio you just burble on,' Daisy pointed out as they pushed through the door into the foyer. 'People forget what they hear two seconds later—I'm sure of it. In fact, I've proof as the same people used to ask the same questions week after week. But with the web-site, I write down answers, and people retain more from reading. They can also print out what I've written, which is really scary because if ever I contradict myself they can—and do—quote something back at me.'

'So what do you do?' Alana sounded intrigued enough for Daisy to set aside the problem of love and answer her.

'I have a lot of stock answers, though I try to word them differently each time so people don't think I'm pressing a key and there's the rote answer.'

'And you don't have one for love?'

Daisy frowned at her persistent friend.

'I have dozens for various aspects of love—or for the things that go wrong in a relationship which is mostly to do with love, but I don't think anyone's asked me how you know you're in love before "Just Asking" came up with it this week.'

Now safely back where they'd started, and at the café, Daisy ordered coffee, waited until Alana had ordered hers, then repeated the question.

'How did *you* know you loved Rory?'

Alana frowned at her.

'I don't know how I knew,' she said, after a silence so long Daisy thought she wasn't going to answer. 'I just knew.'

Then she grinned.

'Oh, I had all the physical symptoms, the melting bones, palpitations, sun shining in the ward when he walked in even if I was nowhere near a window, but I put all that down to lust—with a good dose of frustration thrown in because we couldn't get together. Then I hurt so much for him when he thought he might lose Jason...'

'Hurting for some one you love. I'll put that in. Do you think I should tell JA about the melting bones and palpitations? I usually put that down to lust as well.'

'More attraction than lust, and you have to have attraction as part of the package, surely. The attraction comes first and then as you get to know the person love grows.'

'You two look as if you're having a serious conversation. Can anyone join in?'

It was Rory, one hand dropping lightly onto Alana's shoulder, his fingers tightening in a secret message.

Of love? Daisy wondered as Rory wandered off to order coffee.

But Julian did that to her, and it *wasn't* love.

'Now at least we can get a man's point of view,' Alana said cheerfully, shifting to another chair so Rory could sit between them.

'On what?' he asked, returning in time to hear the remark.

'On love,' Alana said, beaming at her new husband. 'Daisy has a client on her web-site who wants to know how you know you're in love, and we're not sure if it's a he or a she, and we can do the "she" part, but if—what's the name, Daisy?'

'"Just Asking".'

'Right,' Alana continued. 'If "Just Asking" is a man, it would be good if we could give him a male perspective.'

Rory looked slightly confused, but he'd lived in Near West for long enough to have heard similar strange conversations.

'So, how did you know you were in love with me?' Alana prompted, grinning because she knew he'd be embarrassed.

But Rory simply turned to Daisy and smiled.

'It wasn't what you might call instantaneous, though, heaven knows, I was so attracted to her right from the start, it was a wonder I didn't jump her bones very early on. But there were complications and she acted like she hated me, then when I finally worked out she was attracted to me, you mucked that up by telling her it would be disastrous for Jason if we had a relationship.'

He paused to sip his coffee and a far-away look came into his eyes.

'Then one night Jason was going to a social, and he used some stuff of Alana's on his hair, and went mad thinking all his hair would fall out, and she handled him so calmly, yet so lovingly, I knew immediately I wanted her in my life for ever. It was as if a big light had been switched on in the sky, spotlighting what I'd seen but hadn't recognised. I was so stunned, I think I fled her flat and blundered into your place, asking you some inane question about Jason and sex education.'

'I remember that night,' Daisy told him, frowning as she recalled it. 'I must admit, you didn't look like a man in love. You looked more like someone who'd just been sat on by an elephant. Startled, bemused, fairly flattened and not particularly coherent.'

Rory laughed.

'Perfect description of how I felt.'

'Well, that should help "Just Asking",' Alana said, chuckling quietly at the memories. 'Tell him if he ever feels as if an elephant's just sat on him, he'll know for sure.'

The talk switched to other things, Rory asking Daisy about her mother—which reminded her she should be on her way back to the hospital, not discussing love with her friends.

CHAPTER TEN

RETURNING to the hospital, Daisy went first to her mother's room, peering through the glass to see her mother propped up in the bed, alive, alert, smiling at Glen who sat adoringly by her side.

Maybe Julian is right and love isn't all it's cracked up to be, Daisy thought sourly, as this overt display of affection made her stomach squirm.

With a weak, languid hand, her mother waved her in.

'Darling! Glen told me you'd been here.'

She reached out her free hand towards Daisy and, though she sounded bright, Daisy could hear the stress and tiredness in her voice.

She took the offered hand and kissed her mother's cheek.

'You have to rest, you know. And really start looking after yourself.'

Her mother touched her cheek.

'I will,' she promised, then she squeezed Daisy's fingers. 'Just hearing you worrying about me the way you always used to do makes me feel better.'

A nurse appeared, tutting that her patient had two visitors.

'One at a time and restricted visits. This patient needs rest more than company.'

Glen stood up, but Daisy waved to him to stay.

'Mum and I will have plenty of time to catch up when she's convalescing. Now I've seen her, I'd better go to work. You're welcome to stay at my place, Glen. The couch opens up into a bed. I'll drop back later with a key so you can come and go as you please.'

From the hospital to the clinic, although she knew they'd all be ready to leave work. But she was worried about appointments she'd missed this morning, and needed to know what had been done about rescheduling her patients.

'How's your mother?'

The same question was asked by all the staff, but only Julian scanned her face with anxious eyes as he spoke.

'I've seen her, spoken to her,' she replied to Julian, meeting him in the corridor outside his office when the rest of the staff had departed.

Daisy wondered if her eyes, as she studied him in return, looked equally anxious. His arrival at the hospital this morning had thrown her off balance.

'The doctors are confident she'll come through now, but it will be a long convalescence.'

'I'm glad,' Julian said, and he reached out to rest his hand on her shoulder, offering a comforting squeeze.

It was all her taut nerves needed. She all but heard the snap as the tightness broke and certainly felt the moisture on her cheeks as her eyes brimmed, and tears flowed unchecked.

Feeling incredibly foolish, she backed away from Julian, but his grip tightened, preventing escape, and he drew her into his arms.

'Oh, Daisy,' he murmured, holding her very tightly, while she splashed more tears down the front of his shirt.

Eventually, as he had done before, he found a handkerchief, but, instead of offering it to her, he mopped her face.

Julian looked into the red-rimmed eyes and wondered

for the first time if maybe the pain of love was the same as the pain of an ulcer.

If love—romantic love—might actually exist for him.

Right now, his pain was all for Daisy—for the things he'd learned about her life, for the betrayals she'd suffered.

'Glen was your number three?' he asked softly, and she nodded, head bowed to hide her emotions.

'He married your mother?'

Another nod, but this time he needed to see her face, so he took her chin in his hand and tilted her head up to face him.

'Yet you still believe in love?'

'You needn't sound so incredulous,' she snapped, reverting to the Daisy he knew. 'Just because I've had bad luck—or bad judgement—it doesn't negate the fact that people all over the world are falling in love every day. Romantic love, Julian Austin. Garlands of flowers and hearts entwined—the lot!'

She glared at him so fiercely he had to kiss her, and as the kiss deepened and she began to tremble in his arms, his uneasy, unanchored heart began to beat so rapidly he forgot about ulcers and started, in the dim recesses of his mind, to worry about heart attacks instead.

He held her to him, one hand following the taut curve of her buttocks, sliding upwards beneath her loose shirt to feel the silken skin beneath it, pressing her closer to his body, knowing she'd be aware of his need.

'Daisy!'

Her name came out as a muffled groan of desire, but the answering cry—more a whimper than a cry—escalated his excitement, and when she eased her fingers between the buttons of his shirt and pressed them against his skin, fire ripped through his loins.

Kissing her, touching her, being touched and kissed in return, moving at the same time, through the door, across his office, clothes coming off, the lack of suitable furniture no deterrent as he settled on a chair, Daisy clasped in his arms, the two of them adjusting to the fit of each other's body, desperate to repeat the pleasure they'd enjoyed before and reach the ease and relief they'd been denying themselves.

Later, passion spent, she nestled in his arms, and this time her name was nothing more than sigh of breath, a puff of air, a whisper of delight.

'Daisy!'

But soft and heartfelt though it was, Julian instantly regretted it for it broke the spell between them. She pushed back so she could look at him, her cheeks flushed, her dark hair framing a face that looked both startled and bemused.

'No!' she said, the anguish in her voice giving the lie to the denial. 'We can't do this. I won't go through it all again, Julian. Loving someone just to have them walk away.'

She tried to break away from him, but he held her shoulders, feeling the tension in her muscles, seeing the unhappiness in her face.

'I've told you I won't walk away and I mean it, Daisy,' he said, surprised to find his own voice was in working order, considering the tumult in the rest of his body.

'Not physically perhaps—but emotionally?'

She stared defiantly at him.

'Emotionally you wouldn't even be there to start off with, and I couldn't live with that either. I'm sorry, Julian. I know it seemed like a good idea—a marriage that suited both our needs—but it's not for me.'

She hesitated, looking vaguely around as if she'd just discovered where they were. Leaning forward, she picked up his shirt from the floor, then stood up and pulled it around her shoulders, as if needing to be at least partially clothed before she could speak.

'It sounds unutterably stupid but, seeing my mother and Glen together, seeing how they feel about each other, it brought so much home to me. If ever there was a relationship that could have destroyed my belief in love, it was that one. I'd taken him home to meet my mother, Julian, and suddenly I didn't exist. Not for either of them.'

His stomach cramped with pain—again—but this time it was for her.

Daisy sighed, then a small smile wobbled on her lips.

'Seems silly to think they've now confirmed my faith that love exists, doesn't it? But seeing them together...'

Her voice trailed off, and he stood up. She backed against the desk, her body tensing visibly, her eyes issuing a defiant challenge.

As calmly as he could, he gathered up their clothes, setting hers on the desk beside her, being careful not to touch her. Then, behind her back, he pulled on his underwear and trousers, ignoring the shirt she'd now dropped back on the floor.

He waited until she was dressed, then once again broke the silence with her name.

'Daisy?'

This time it was a plea.

'No, Julian, it wouldn't work. It doesn't matter how sexually compatible we are, it's not enough for me.'

'And the baby you want?' The harsh demand seemed to shock her, and she pressed her hands to her stomach.

'I've changed my mind,' she said bluntly. 'I've realised how selfish it would be of me to have a child for my own fulfillment and gratification, yet offer that child only half a life—half a family.'

He stepped back, as if the words had been a physical blow—a slap in the face.

'But, Daisy, you'd thought that through. You know a child can grow up happy and well adjusted with one loving parent—you've argued that through with me more than once.'

He hesitated, then added, 'Don't let what's happened between us spoil your dream.'

He wanted to touch her so badly his arms ached, but he held back, waiting, though for what he didn't know. And in the end, after the clear, grey-green eyes had studied him for a long moment, she simply shook her head and moved away, walking out of the room as if the passion that had flared again between them had never been.

Daisy's resignation hit Julian's desk a week later and, though he now knew her well enough to understand argument would be useless, he still stormed into her office, demanding an explanation.

'It's in the letter,' she said calmly. 'My mother's coming out of hospital, Glen has to go back to work, but she can't be left on her own. I'm going back to the coast with them for an indefinite period of time.'

Disbelief acted as a detonator for his rage.

'To live with the man you once loved and the mother who betrayed you?' The words exploded from his lips.

'At least they're human,' she shot back, 'with feelings and emotions, not just a brain that rationalises everything to death. At least they believe in love!'

She stood up, whisked a pile of papers off her desk, shoved them into her briefcase and added, 'As I explained in my letter, Chelsea's over her morning sickness and is happy to come back to work. She starts tomorrow.'

'So, you're really going?' How pathetic he sounded.

So much so she didn't bother answering, merely clutched her briefcase to her chest and walked out.

Daisy settled her mother on the couch in the living room and handed her the television remote control so she could switch between the daytime soaps she loved to watch.

This was escape time, when Daisy could retire to her bedroom, check her web-site, answer emails and generally forget just how irritable her mother always had, and still did, make her feel.

Naturally, the first question on her web-site was about love. From "Just Asking" again.

'All right, Daisy,' 'Just Asking' began. 'I think I've got the symptoms you mentioned and a few thousand others as well, but what do I do next? How do I tell her?'

Daisy shook her head. The man—it had to be a man as only a man would be so persistent—was hopeless.

'I don't know, JA,' she told the screen. 'I really don't know.'

But he needed an answer, so she frowned at the screen for a little longer, then began to write, letting her fingers type the words in before her brain had time to censor them.

'Just tell her,' she began. 'Stop dithering and come right out and say it. Say, "I love you", and be done with it.'

She banged her finger on the send button and turned to question two.

Another love query.

Lately it seemed as if it was all anyone was thinking about. Personally, she was beginning to wonder why she'd ever set such store by it. Bad enough that Glen and her mother canoodled in front of her every evening, but it was honeymoon season as well, and if she escaped for a quiet walk along the beach, she inevitably tripped over a couple kissing on the sand, or ran into them in the shadows of the pandanus palms that lined the dunes.

No, the longer she stayed, the more she came to believe Julian might have a point—that it was nothing more than a chemical reaction raised to lofty heights by poets, song-writers and commercial interests.

But just thinking of Julian made Daisy's heart ache and her eyes water, and if that wasn't love, what was it?

She looked at the question and sighed, then, because she wasn't up to any more love today, checked the next one.

'Kisses for Free' wanted to know if she could get any diseases just kissing boys. She liked kissing, she went on to explain, and didn't see the harm in it, but could she catch something?

Only love, Daisy thought, but she answered sensibly, then moved on to a woman who'd been adopted and had now found her birth mother. She wanted Daisy's advice on how to handle their first meeting.

It took her a long time to say very little, simply warning the woman that such meetings didn't always gel at first, and getting to know her birth mother would be the same as getting to know any other stranger. She urged 'Adopted' to go into the meeting with an open mind, without any thought for the past and what had happened, but with hope for the future—they might eventually become friends.

Adoption? Wouldn't that have been easier than getting involved with Julian? It was hard these days, especially for a single person, but still possible, so why had she somehow fallen under his spell and gone along, even for an instant, with his marriage of convenience idea?

Because you liked the way he smiled, she reminded herself. Right from the start!

She scrolled back up to the ignored question about love. 'My girlfriend and I are madly in love and want to get married, but my mother says love doesn't last and we need more than that to get married—like money! Is she right?'

'Yes!' Daisy answered bluntly, and she was about to let it go at that when she relented, adding that the fewer outside pressures on the marriage—pressures like not knowing where the rent money was coming from—the more chance it had of success. 'You only have to look at the divorce rates to know nearly fifty per cent of marriages fail.'

She sent the message then absent-mindedly tapped a few keys, wondering where on the World Wide Web she'd find the information she sought—statistical evidence of the success or otherwise of arranged marriages.

'Don't be ridiculous,' she told herself, but the more evenings she spent with the lovebirds, the more cynical she knew she was becoming.

So, discovering she was pregnant on the evening she finally returned to her flat and took the test in the privacy of her own bathroom threw her into less turmoil than she'd have expected. For a start, the warm snuggly feeling beneath her breastbone returned at the thought of a baby, while considering the option of giving it two parents brought tingling sensations to many other parts of her body.

Mentally listing all the reasons marriage to Julian would be good—the baby would have two parents, she enjoyed his company and her body need never ache with frustration for him again—she debated how to tell him, then realised she hadn't seen him for three weeks and when last she had, not long after they'd shared an unexpected but surprisingly passionate encounter, she rather thought she might have been very insulting.

Besides, in three weeks he might have proposed to someone else.

Actually, considering his behaviour with herself and Ingrid, he could have proposed to—quick moment of mathematical calculation—forty-two women since then.

A squelchy feeling in her stomach that had nothing to do with being pregnant warned her that the road ahead could be rocky, but she had to do what she had to do.

For a start, she had to tell him—to hide the news would be dishonest, particularly as he so wanted to have a child.

Then she could give him the option of having regular contact with the child...

Or?

Marrying her?

Oh, dear, what if he didn't want to?

Knowing that any further thought or procrastination would lead to panic stations, she squared her shoulders, opened the front door, marched across the foyer and pressed the button for the lift.

Then procrastination won and she decided to walk up the stairs. Exercise was good for the baby. She'd tell Julian and see what happened. Let him make the next move.

She was so geared up for the confrontation—so wired

with apprehension—that when Madeleine opened the front door Daisy simply stared at her.

'Oh, Daisy, you're back. Let me give you a hug. I can't tell you how grateful I am to you for all the help you gave Julian and Mum.'

She enveloped Daisy in a warm embrace.

'Come in, come in. How's your mother? I've just put the twins to bed so we can have a drink. And I've got a present for you. It's a touristy thing but I thought you might like it.'

Madeleine bustled her into the apartment, headed her towards a chair, then disappeared. And without needing to be told, Daisy knew Julian was no longer living there.

Why would he be, with Madeleine and Graham back home? Heavens, they must have been back for weeks. What was she thinking, blundering up here like this?

'Here!'

Madeleine returned, beaming with delight as she handed Daisy an exquisitely wrapped parcel.

Daisy untied the ribbon, then unwrapped the gift, exclaiming in surprise and genuine delight at the small enamelled daisy brooch.

The phone rang as Daisy pinned it on her shirt, and Madeleine, who'd been helping with the catch, said casually, 'That will be Julian. He phones every night at this time to find out if you're back.'

As if jolted by an electric shock, Daisy shot out of her chair, beat Madeleine across the room and put her hand down firmly on the receiver.

'What do you mean, he rings every night?' she demanded, above the clangour of the phone.

'To see if you're home,' Madeleine repeated patiently. Then she shrugged. 'I suppose he wants to know when you're going back to work. You were working with him, weren't you?'

It seemed a reasonable enough explanation, and the excitement that had briefly skittered through her heart died down. Or maybe it was the cessation of noise from the phone, and nothing to do with her heart.

'Now I'll have to dial caller ID,' Madeleine said crossly. 'Why didn't you want me to talk to him?'

Daisy shrugged, then, because she really wanted to see Julian but also wanted the advantage of surprise, she sought refuge in a lie.

'I haven't decided if I want to go back to work,' she said. 'You don't need to lie to him, just don't call him back.'

Madeleine gave her a strange look but said nothing, and Daisy guessed that if Julian rang again, she'd tell him what had happened.

'Where's he living?' she asked, hoping she sounded far more casual than she felt.

Madeleine grinned at her.

'In Alana's flat,' she said.

Daisy shook her head.

'But that doesn't make sense,' she protested. 'If he's living there, why should he phone you to see if I've come back?'

Madeleine seemed puzzled by the question.

'In case he missed you coming in?' she guessed. The she shrugged. 'I've never really thought to ask him.'

Daisy sighed. Now Madeleine was back—right here in front of her—it was harder than ever to believe she and Julian could have come out of the same gene pool.

She thanked Madeleine again for the brooch and departed, walking back down the stairs, not for exercise for the well-being of her child but to prolong the time before she faced him.

Noises from beyond the door told her he was home and, afraid if she delayed any longer she'd lose her nerve, she raised her hand and knocked.

He opened the door and for a moment stared at her as if she were a mirage, then he smiled and Daisy relaxed—just slightly.

'You're back,' he said, and because the smile had faded and her tension returned, and with it all the skittering nervous manifestations of her attraction to this man, her mouth went dry and she had to make do with a nod.

'Do you want to come in?'

He pulled the door further open and waved his hand towards the living room.

'No, I just came to tell you—I just called in—I don't have to see you now...'

His hands rested on her shoulders, causing more physical problems, and the smile returned, a gentle, teasing version of it this time.

'Come in, I've coffee brewing. The animals have gone, transferred to Alana's and Rory's new house. Did you hear about the house? It's on a couple of acres not far from Alex's mother's place.'

Daisy looked at him and shook her head, but she went in and sat down in an armchair.

'Don't tell me you've been getting into all the togetherness of Near West,' she mocked, pleased to have a neutral subject to discuss.

The smile widened.

'They're nice people,' he admitted. 'And as I look like being here for a while—Madeleine and Graham have also bought a house so I'm shifting up there—I thought I'd better start being neighbourly.'

He's shifting into the penthouse with the spa, Daisy thought, and her hand went protectively to her stomach, because she knew that's when the baby must have been conceived. Their other encounter was too recent for a test to prove positive.

'So, did you want to see me about something in particular?'

The question reminded her of her mission, but now she was here—and he was here—she didn't have a clue what to say.

I'm pregnant.

Do you still want to marry me?

Would it be convenient to arrange that marriage now?

As fast as the sentences formed she discarded them, and when they stopped forming, she simply stared at him, looking up into his face, aware her eyes were probably wide with desperation.

'Daisy?'

It was a question, but gently asked. At the same time, he dropped to squat beside the chair and take her hands.

'Is everything all right? Is your mother OK?'

She felt the pressure of his fingers and returned it, clinging to his hands as if they were her lifeline to sanity.

'She's fine, we're having a baby.'

The words rushed out, all on top of each other, so it seemed to take an age before Julian actually heard them.

She knew the instant he caught on because he dropped her hands as if they'd burnt him and backed away.

He's horrified, she realised, and tears began to form behind her eyes.

'Ah!' he said, when she'd blinked them back and steeled herself for his rejection.

'So!' he added, and though she searched and searched she could see no glimmer of a smile on his usually smiling face.

Then his shoulders rose as he took in a deep breath and dropped into the chair opposite her—out of touching distance.

'And what do you want to do about it?' he asked.

Still no smile, and his voice was so cool they might have been discussing a patient.

Actually, he'd probably care more about a patient...

'Daisy?'

She glared at him.

'I heard you,' she snapped. 'I just don't know how to answer. I wanted to ask first. I wanted to ask you what *you* wanted to do about it.'

Julian nodded his head.

'All right, I'll consider myself asked.'

He studied her for a moment, then he answered, very quietly, very carefully and so gently Daisy heard his voice caress her skin.

'You've already ruled out a loveless marriage, but would you consider a love match?'

It was so unbelievable Daisy snorted.

'With you?' she demanded, angry with his teasing and with herself for making such a botch of things. 'The man who thinks love is something dreamed up in an advertising agency? Actually, after three weeks with my mother, I'm inclined to believe you. I'm changing sides from emotional to rational thinking and, that being the case, the mutually convenient arrangement might just work.'

'Oh, I don't think so,' Julian said calmly, and Daisy felt her jaw drop open in disbelief.

'Well, that's OK!' she said, standing up and storming

towards the door. 'I was always prepared to do this on my own.'

Julian's strides were longer than hers, and he reached her destination before she did.

'Are you sure I can't persuade you to change your mind?' he asked, and the shivers of awareness she'd been trying to ignore became trembles of desire. 'About the love match, that is,' he murmured, his eyes fixed on her lips, his head dropping lower, so Daisy was mesmerised into remaining where she was until his mouth claimed hers.

'Oh, Daisy,' he muttered, as his lips delivered hungry kisses and demanded she respond. 'If only you knew how I've missed you. How I've longed to hold you like this—to kiss you again.'

The words, made disjointed by the kissing, rattled around in her head, taking a while to sort themselves into a logical if unbelievable sequence.

But before she could respond, or question, he was talking again.

'You taught me how to love, showed me how with the love you gave to others, teased me into learning it, then walked away,' he said, nuzzling his face into her hair while his hands pressed against the contours of her back as if needing to know every inch of her through touch alone. 'So now, Daisy Rutherford, if it's marriage you want, it has to be a love match.'

He lifted his head and looked down into her eyes.

'Well?'

Her heart was full to bursting but she was afraid to believe. She looked at the man who held her, the man with the easy smile that hid a childhood deprived of love—the man with eyes like the deep ocean at the end of the pier, eyes that were now reaffirming his words.

And couldn't resist teasing.

'You mean love with garlands of flowers and hearts entwined? The whole commercialised entity?'

'Wretch!' he murmured, and dropped another, oh, so light kiss on her lips. 'No, I don't mean that at all. I mean love that shines between us so brightly it reaches out and touches not only our children but our family and friends. Love that fills our lives, to comfort us in bad times and excite us in the good. I've tried for years to rationalise it, Daisy, but you knocked away all my pretensions and left an empty shell that can only be filled by a woman with grey-green eyes and a cloud of dark hair, and the capacity to enfold all those dear to her in her own sweet brand of love.'

Daisy touched his face in wonder.

'You mean it,' she murmured, afraid to speak too loudly in case the spell was broken.

Julian's faced creased into a so-familiar smile, and he swung her into his arms and whirled her around.

'You'd better believe it,' he told her, as he set her back on her feet. 'Though I admit I was so confused at first I had to ask an expert.'

The teasing twinkle in his eyes started a tinkle of bells in her head. Hadn't Alana said ask an expert with a website? JA? Julian Austin? Surely not!

But by then he was kissing her again so they didn't talk at all for a long time.

EPILOGUE

'THAT dress is perfect,' Gabi said to Kirsten, as the two of them sat on Daisy's sofa a month later and watched Alana twist a garland of tiny orchids into Daisy's dark hair.

'She's not as anti-shopping as some people,' teased Kirsten. 'Heaven knows what you must have been like, getting your dress. Daisy would have tried on everything I suggested, only this one was the first and it was perfect on her.'

Gabi sighed. She could barely remember fitting into something with a waist.

'There!' Alana said, and turned Daisy so she faced the two friends on the sofa. 'What do you think?'

'Beautiful,' they chorused, and Daisy blushed.

'Y-you've all b-been wonderful,' she stuttered, excitement all but choking her. 'Julian and I didn't intend this, you know. We were eloping, like Alana and Rory.'

'No way,' Kirsten said firmly. 'That pair deprived us of one wedding, and though we'll miss the wedding part of yours, we're not missing out on the party. Or seeing you as a bride.'

Daisy glanced towards the gilded mirror in the entry foyer of her flat.

'I don't look too bridal, do I?' she asked anxiously. 'I mean, we have to trail through the hospital—I don't want to look too obvious.'

'You look just right,' Alana assured her, while Gabi found her eyes misting as she nodded agreement. In a filmy dress in varying shades of lavender and lilac, Daisy was hardly a conventional bride, but the colours enhanced her beauty, already heightened by the glow of love.

But Daisy still fretted, not convinced the special dress wasn't too much for a quiet wedding ceremony. A tap on the door told her Julian had arrived.

'I think I'm panicking,' she said to her friends, holding her hands out in front of her and watching them shake.

'No, you're not,' Alana said firmly. 'You're simply overwhelmingly excited about the wonderful step you're about to take.'

Then Julian was there, Kirsten having answered his knock, and the glow of admiration and love in his eyes put all her fears to rest. He reached out his hand, and she took it, remembering as she did what he'd said to her the night before.

'We're already committed to each other, Daisy, in every way that counts. The ceremony is for others, not for us.'

To a chorus of 'Good luck' and 'See you later' they left the flat, taking the lift down to the basement.

Julian held tightly to Daisy's hand, and though he seemed about to speak several times, in the end he said nothing. Which suited Daisy as her vocal cords were so constricted by nerves she'd not have been able to answer.

In the end, the normality of it all calmed her. Driving to the hospital together, Julian pulling into the familiar parking space, walking to the lift—where the usual group of people waiting to go either up or down did give her strange looks—then up to Paediatrics and into a ward bright with streamers and balloons.

'Happy wedding,' the ambulatory children, gathered in the play area, all chorused, and Daisy relaxed. It felt so right to be getting married here—and getting married to Julian—that the tension she'd been feeling gave way to a wave of elation.

The celebrant waited by Bella's bed—a Bella barely recognisable, dressed in a lavender fairy costume she'd chosen herself from a toy-shop catalogue. Instead of a posy, she held a fairy wand, which she waved excitedly as Daisy and Julian approached.

Bella's parents, down for the weekend, had agreed to be witnesses and, with Bella as a fairy flower-girl, Daisy and Julian were married.

'It's not over yet,' Julian murmured to her as, the ceremony and small celebration with the children complete, they finally left the ward.

'No,' Daisy said, pressing close against her husband's side as they waited for the lift. 'But at least we've still got your flat to escape to if the party in the penthouse goes on too long.'

She sighed, then added, 'I'm sorry about the party, but you know Gabi and Kirsten and Alana. Once they get an idea in their heads, they're impossible to stop.'

Julian smiled at her.

'Add my mother and Madeleine to that list and you've got a force capable of moving mountains. And having the party in the penthouse meant your mother could attend, if only for a short time and with the least possible effort to her.'

Daisy shook her head, once again bemused by the understanding and compassion of the man she'd just married. Julian had arranged for her mother to stay overnight with Madeleine, so she *could* attend the celebration for a short time.

The love Daisy felt for him all but overwhelmed her, but she waited until they reached the car, then she stopped him before he bent to open the door for her.

'You're wonderful,' she said quietly, hoping he'd hear the depth of sincerity in her words. 'A really special man!'

Julian looked surprised, then he smiled—the warm, all-enveloping smile she now knew he kept, in his repertoire of smiles, especially for her.

'No,' he said, shaking his head to add to the denial. 'I'm just an ordinary man who's had the extraordinary luck to find and fall in love with a very special woman.'

He took her hand.

'I'm glad you said something, because although I might have gabbled out the odd sentence, and hopefully made all the right responses in the ceremony, for the last hour I've been as close to tongue-tied as I've ever been. I walked into your flat, and there you were, looking so beautiful it took my breath away. I wanted to say something—to tell you—but no words would come.'

He bent and kissed her gently on the lips.

'I love you, Daisy Austin, more than life itself.'

Then he kissed her again and added, 'To think that deciding to have a baby could lead to all of this.'

LIVE THE EMOTION

Modern Romance™
...seduction and
passion guaranteed

Tender Romance™
...love affairs that
last a lifetime

Medical Romance™
...medical drama
on the pulse

Historical Romance™
...rich, vivid and
passionate

Sensual Romance™
...sassy, sexy and
seductive

Blaze Romance™
...the temperature's
rising

27 new titles every month.

Live the emotion

MILLS & BOON®

MILLS & BOON

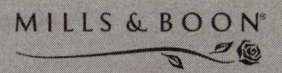

Medical Romance™

TO THE DOCTOR A DAUGHTER by *Marion Lennox*

Dr Nate Ethan has all he needs – a job he loves as a country doctor and a bachelor lifestyle. Dr Gemma Campbell is about to change all that! Her sister has left her with two children – and one of them is Nate's. She must give Nate his baby and walk away – but Nate finds he will do anything to stop her leaving…

A MOTHER'S SPECIAL CARE by *Jessica Matthews*

Dr Mac Grant is struggling as a single dad with a demanding career. Juggling is proving difficult, and he is aware of his son's longing for a mother. Lori Ames is a nurse on Mac's ward – a single mother with a beautiful daughter of her own. Can she bestow upon them the special care that both children so desperately need?

RESCUING DR MacALLISTER by *Sarah Morgan*

A&E nurse Ellie Harrison is intrigued by the ruggedly handsome new doctor at Ambleside. But Dr Ben MacAllister is playing it cool. The pace and excitement of the A&E department thrusts them together and reveals that Ben's growing attraction is as strong as hers – then Ellie realises he has a secret…

On sale 2nd May 2003

Available at most branches of WH Smith, Tesco, Martins, Borders, Eason, Sainsbury's and all good paperback bookshops.

MILLS & BOON

Medical Romance™

DR DEMETRIUS'S DILEMMA by Margaret Barker

Eight years ago Dr Demetrius Petros and Staff Nurse Chloe Metcalfe had a passionate affair on the beautiful Greek island of Ceres. It ended when a devastated Chloe returned to England, believing he had never really loved her. Now they are working together — and it's as if they have never been apart...

THE SURGEON'S GIFT by Carol Marinelli

Sister Rachael Holroyd has returned to Melbourne City hospital after a traumatic year away — yet the new plastic surgeon manages to make her heart flutter and she finds herself falling for him fast! Dr Hugh Connell is as gifted as he is gorgeous — and he just knows he can help Rachael get over her troubled past...

THE NURSE'S CHILD by Abigail Gordon

GP Richard Haslett isn't looking for a wife, and has promised his adopted daughter never to replace her mother. However, he finds himself drawn to Freya Farnham, the new Resident Nurse at Amelia's school. Then he discovers that Freya is Amelia's real mother...

On sale 2nd May 2003

Available at most branches of WH Smith, Tesco, Martins, Borders, Eason, Sainsbury's and all good paperback bookshops.

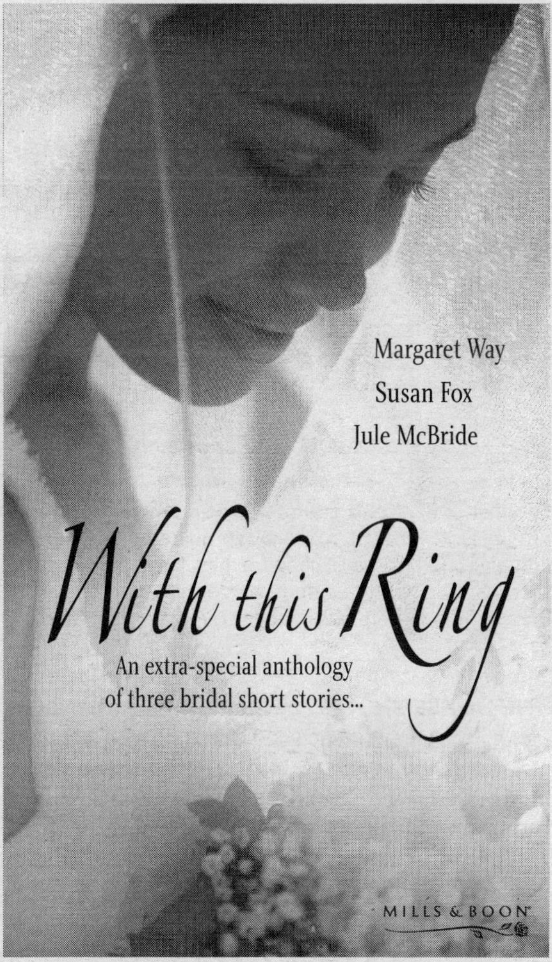
Margaret Way
Susan Fox
Jule McBride
With this Ring
An extra-special anthology
of three bridal short stories...
MILLS & BOON

MILLS & BOON

DON'T MISS...

MILLS & BOON

BETTY NEELS

LAST APRIL FAIR
& THE COURSE OF TRUE LOVE

THE ULTIMATE COLLECTION

VOLUME TEN

On sale 4th April 2003

Available at most branches of WH Smith, Tesco, Martins, Borders, Eason, Sainsbury's and all good paperback bookshops.